THE KEYS TO FANNY

Dear Marilyn -

from one
writer to another -
best writing
wishes.
Sally

SALLY WAHL CONSTAIN

ISBN: 1494928787
ISBN 13: 9781494928780
Library of Congress Control Number: 2014900425
CreateSpace Independent Publishing Platform
North Charleston, South Carolina

Dedicated to my grandsons, Robby and Gregory Constain,
and to children everywhere.
May they always have choices in their lives,
and may they choose wisely and well.

TABLE OF CONTENTS

$\mathcal{O}$ N E

Sunday, October 22, 1896

I wake up thinking about last year. I'm thirteen today, and I wish I could turn time all the way back to my twelfth birthday, before things began to change.

I pause outside Mama's door and listen to her low moans. Last year when I passed this room, I could hear Mama and Papa talking quietly. The gentle rise and fall of their voices made me feel safe. I was never allowed to go inside, but now it is expected of me. Papa has been sleeping on the couch in his study, and Mama's thin body barely leaves an impression in her plump feather bed.

I hold my breath and push the door open. I tiptoe over to the window and open it a crack. The cool October air whistles into the room, and Mama moves a little. I open it more to let out the stale, sickly smell.

"Fanny, Aunt Freda will be here soon." Mama's voice is low and sort of shaky. "Happy birthday, sweet child." She looks straight into my teary eyes and holds my hand. Her fingers are like icicles. What has happened to the strong, steady hands that kneaded the dough every Friday at dawn, braided the challah at noon, and blessed the Sabbath candles at dusk? My hands are growing into these and other responsibilities.

I hear Aunt Freda burst in the front door. The huge green sack she carries with her everywhere is stuffed with goodies. My aunt's massive arms embrace and push me at the same time. "Come along, Birthday Girl, and try on your present," she orders. Aunt Freda has made me a new outfit, with fabric from Papa's store, of course. The pink linen blouse has a high ruffled neck that tickles my chin. The blue shell buttons close gently down the front and on the cuffs of the long sleeves. They match the full skirt, which falls to my ankles. "Just right, Fanny, you're a real young lady, now!" Aunt Freda leaves me in front of the hall mirror and hurries to help her sister wash and dress.

I look at myself from head to toe. This is the perfect gift. Last year's clothes are too small. Everything is changing. *Slow down*, I scream in my head.

I should be helping in the kitchen. I should be setting the table for lunch. Instead, I'm sitting in the parlor, sitting in the chair that Mama no longer uses. Aunt Freda said to relax, to enjoy my special day. I lean back carefully, so I don't wrinkle my new clothes. I would never wear such a pretty blouse to cook and serve in. For that, Mama and I wear housedresses and long aprons. I guess I'll start using Mama's soon. She's too weak to do anything at all, and I'm growing up very fast, much too fast.

Everyone says that Mama was the best cook in the family, maybe in our whole village. She taught Manya and me all her wonderful dishes. We learned to make golden chicken soup simmering with thick slices of carrot and slippery noodles, flaky potato knishes, and warm apple turnovers, my favorite. Mama always talked as we worked, so the recipes entered our hands and heads at the same time. Nothing could be written down, because girls do not go to school and are never taught to read and write. "Leave that to the boys," Papa says. "Learn to cook like Mama, and you'll get a good husband."

Sometimes, when I roll out the dough for the strudel, I see my life rolling away from me. I picture myself as a ball, rolling out the door, rolling under the canopy to wed, and then to my chosen husband's home and kitchen. And bed. Later, somehow, babies will arrive. The little boys will go to school. The girls will go to the kitchen, and on and on.

I feel sleepy. I close my eyes and begin to drift off. The sounds around me are like faraway music. I hear Louie's sweet voice reciting his lessons in Papa's study. Papa's deep voice praises and corrects. I hear Aunt Freda's strong voice blending with Mama's gentle one. From time to time, I even hear Mama laugh a little and then start to cough.

I once heard Papa asking Mama about Aunt Freda and Uncle Avram. "Who would match such a lively woman with a sickly old man? What was your Papa thinking?" Mama lowered her voice, so that all I could hear was something about a problem with the first match somehow involving a letter. Strange.

I'm wondering what really happened, and I'm wondering who will be chosen for me, and when. What if Mama is not here to help with the choice? Will Papa make a mistake like my grandpa did with Aunt Freda? Is there a way for me to stop the rolling? My head is spinning with questions.

*I'm helping Aunt Freda to clear the table, while Manya guides Mama back to bed. Papa and Jacob go to the shop to talk about business. I like to chat with Aunt Freda while we work.

Most people think I'm shy, or just unfriendly. Mama always says that it's just my way. Last year, Cousin Chava came to tell Mama that she's concerned about me being much too quiet. I was pleased when Mama stood up, took her guest's arm, and walked her toward the door, saying, "Fanny will be fine. She's stronger than anyone imagines. Now, go home, Chava, and worry about your own daughters."

I could always count on Mama. Now, she counts on me. Who can *I* count on? Papa is always working and very nervous about Mama's illness when he's here. Manya and Jacob live in the next village, and Louie's at school all day. If only I could go, too.

Aunt Freda finishes washing the dishes and gets ready to leave. "Uncle Avram has been alone all day, Fanny. His cousin Sophie sent him medicine from New York. I have some for your mama. Save it for when the pain is very bad." Aunt Freda reaches deep into her green bag and pulls out a thick square of paper, tied in string. "Put it away, Fanny. You're in charge now. You'll know what to do." Aunt Freda looks me straight in the eyes. "I'm counting on you, Fanny." The door closes behind her and then opens again. Aunt Freda hugs me and whispers in my ear, "And you can count on me, too... always."

I untie the cord, push the paper aside, and find a brown bottle filled with liquid. I slip it carefully into the third drawer, in between my nightshirts. The papers fall to the floor, and I bend down to pick them up. I stuff them into my apron pocket and head back to the kitchen to make Mama's tea.

Louie is sitting at the table, holding his head in his hands. I can see that he's worried, too. Louie's only ten, and he's about to lose his mama. "Louie," I say, "let's look at these magazine pages that Aunt Freda had in her bag. They're from New York, from Uncle Avram's cousin."

We sit close together and stare hard at each page, as if we're trying to get a good look at another life. "Louie, look at the horses and carriages filled with people. I wonder where they're going. The road is so wide. America looks so big, and really different." The next page is just a jumble of marks—letters and words. Louie tells me that it's not Hebrew or Yiddish. It even looks different than the papers that some of the Russians read.

Their girls don't go to school, either. Sometimes I see them at the market, helping their mothers, too. Actually, we don't mix with them, but I think we're more alike than different. I wish everyone would understand that, and there wouldn't be so much trouble between us. It's very scary.

Louie sees that he can't read the words. Maybe now he knows how I feel. He puts that page aside. "Look at this one, Fanny. An American classroom, and with girls, too! Wow, boys and girls together, studying." I can see he's surprised, and so am I. The children seem to be my age. They all have open books in front of them. The teacher is a tall woman, standing in the front of the room, using a long stick to point at writing on the wall. One girl has her hand raised. She's pretty, with long brown hair like mine, but it's tied up with a ribbon.

I hear Manya come into the kitchen, take the glass of tea, and return to Mama. I slip the classroom picture into my pocket and leave Louie to look at the rest of the papers. As I finish straightening up in the kitchen, the picture of that one girl stays in my head. Imagine, going to school every day, learning to read and write. It would be great. I could read to Mama while she rests. I could make up stories and write them down. I could write Mama's recipes and her stories, too. I could read them to Louie's children one day, or my own, if I should marry. Maybe in America, a girl has a choice about that.

I shake my head to stop this impossible thinking. My hair comes loose and falls over my eyes. Manya closes Mama's door quietly and tiptoes over to me. "I almost forgot, Fanny, here's your gift." I open the small package and watch a rainbow of ribbons spread out across the table. I pick up a yellow one and tie my hair back with it. I run to the hall mirror to have a look. The American schoolgirl stares back at me.

I thank Manya and kiss her good-bye. Then, I gather up my pretty ribbons and put them and my dreams away for another day.

The hall mirror is covered with a sheet. My birth-day ribbons are in my third drawer, along with the American classroom picture and the empty brown bottle. I'm sitting on a low bench in the dining room, between Manya and Aunt Freda. Louie is with the men in the parlor, also sitting on hard seats. The neighbors are preparing food and serving everyone. We are the mourners. We sit for seven days, receiving well-wishers. I'm saying thank you to each person who offers words of sympathy, but I don't really see them. Everything is a haze.

It's been two days since Mama's funeral and three since Aunt Freda arrived with her traveling bag. I was glad and sad to see her. I knew why she'd come. Mama's end was near. I needed her company, and Mama needed more help than I could provide.

"I think I'll be here for a while," she'd said. "Uncle Avram's sister is staying with him. Now give me the bottle, Fanny." The liquid in the brown bottle was almost gone. The medicine had helped Mama sleep each night, until she would wake up gasping for breath and screaming in pain. She could no longer eat or sit up. Most of the time, she didn't know who we were. Poor Mama. Poor us.

"Just enough left." Aunt Freda pocketed the bottle and handed me the market basket. "Leave this with Mrs. Posner. Tell her we'll need it filled with eggs and delivered tomor-row. Take your brother with you, and buy yourselves some sweets." Aunt Freda placed a few coins on the table and went into Mama's room.

I rushed to the door with Louie. It felt good to be out in the crisp November air, even if only for a short time and on a bittersweet errand. We were halfway to town when I remembered the candy money. I handed the basket to Louie. "Wait here, I'll be back right away."

I ran home and through the kitchen door. As I reached for the money, I heard Aunt Freda talking to her sister in a voice I had never heard before, very quiet and sure. "Shira, love, sleep in peace." I peeked through the crack in the door and watched as my aunt let the empty bottle drop to the floor. I saw her remove Mama's pillows from under her head, and I went to meet Louie.

⟨⟩

The eggs were delivered the next morning. They were boiled and served with bagels right after the burial. Round foods are supposed to remind us of the circle of life. I'm tired of sitting on this wooden bench for so long. I'd rather be busy. My head hurts, and my legs are stiff. I feel sleepy. I hear the door open again. A cold gust of air hits me between my eyes, and I look up. *Uh-oh. It's her.* Her voice cracks the air. "Manya, Fanny, your mother was a wonderful woman, a jewel. It's so sad. You know, I arranged her marriage almost twenty years ago. It was a good match. That's why she called on me last year for Manya. You'll be next, Fanny. You look a lot like Shira, and I hear you're a great cook, too. That's good. Freda, how's your dear husband faring these days?" Mrs. Brodsky goes to the parlor to see Papa, leaving a chill in the air.

⟨⟩

"Mama, I'm so cold."
"I know, child, winter's coming. It will be long and hard, but then spring will appear. That's a good season for you, Fanny."

Mama looks pretty. She's sitting on a cloud. Her long brown hair falls to her shoulders. Her cheeks are rosy again. She smiles and reaches out to me. "Rest now, Fanny, and I'll tell you some of your favorite stories. Later, you can write them down."

"Mama, don't you remember? Only boys go to school."

"Your time will come."

"When, Mama, when?"

"Fanny, Fanny, wake up! You're screaming." Aunt Freda is holding a cool dishtowel on my forehead. For a moment, I think it's a pillow covering my face, and I try to push it away.

*A*unt Freda stayed until my fever broke and I was able to take over the household chores. Shiva is over. The neighbors are back in their own kitchens, and Papa has reopened his shop. Louie is in school, and I am home alone. Sometimes I look at the photo of the American classroom and wish I were there. Mama always said that timing is everything, and right now I need to be just where I am.

Each day has its own rhythm. I rise early to prepare breakfast for Papa and Louie. Later I cook, clean, wash, and mend. There is no one to talk to me while I do these things, so I keep Mama's voice in my head all the time.

At noon, I bring Papa his lunch and stay awhile if he's not busy. Papa, Louie, and I have dinner together almost every night. Mama's empty chair sits in the corner, as if waiting for her to return it to her rightful place at the table. Mama's sickbed has been aired out and has fresh linens, but Papa still spends the night in his study. We are doing the best we can, and life goes on.

When Louie and I go to the marketplace on Thursday afternoons, we hear the latest news. There is talk about raids against nearby Jewish settlements, where homes are set ablaze, and villages are destroyed by local ruffians. Everyone here seems to know someone who was hurt or killed in one of these pogroms. We pray that this will not happen here. People who have family members to send for them are packing up and leaving for such faraway places as Argentina, Canada, and America.

Several girls of my age are already being promised in marriage at some future date. I'm not too surprised to see Mrs. Brodsky in Papa's shop one day. I am glad to hear Papa tell her that he's not yet ready for a conversation with her.

⌒

*I*t's exactly one year to the day since Mama died. Last night, we lit the *yahrtzeit* memorial candle, which will burn for one full day. Papa and Louie are at the synagogue saying special prayers.

I'm preparing lunch for the family. I'm making noodle pudding just the way Mama taught me. I add creamy pot cheese and sour cream to the freshly made egg noodles and season it with salt, pepper, and cinnamon.

My sister and her husband arrive just as I pull the bubbling casserole out of the oven. "Mmm, just what I've been craving." Manya rubs her rounded tummy. "We have news, Fanny, but let's wait for Papa." Aunt Freda comes in through the kitchen door and calls me over to her. "Fanny," she whispers, "I have news, too, but don't tell anyone yet. We'll talk after lunch."

Papa takes his seat at the head of the table, clears his throat, and looks at each of us before speaking. "The period of mourning for Shira is complete. We shall observe this date every year, wherever we are. May her memory be for a blessing, and may each of you continue to lead your lives in ways that would make her proud."

Papa is pleased to know he'll become a grandfather next spring. I see tears spring into Manya's eyes. "Papa, your grandchild will be born in Palestine. We'll be leaving in a few weeks to join Jacob's brothers. Life will be safer there, we hope."

Papa breaks the long silence. "Go in peace, and God willing, we'll all join you there one day." He pauses, and then he stands. "Now, I have some news, too. Mrs. Brodsky is coming tomorrow to speak about—"

"*No!*" I run into my room, knocking over the chair. I hide under my covers.

I hear Aunt Freda's footsteps outside my room. I'm wondering about her news. I peek out from under my quilt. Then I hear stronger steps...Papa's.

"Stay out, Freda, leave her be."

"She needs me."

"What she needs is room to grow. I've let you coddle her this past year. Enough! I don't want you to keep filling her head with foolish ideas. There may soon be changes here. Go home to your husband, Freda."

Aunt Freda doesn't respond to Papa. Instead, she calls out, "I'll be back soon, Fanny."

Papa pushes my door open but doesn't come in. "Fanny, you can stay in here today, if you wish. Manya will finish clearing up. I'm leaving on a business trip tomorrow afternoon and will return on Thursday. You and I will talk then."

"I'm sorry, Papa, but I don't want—"

"Not now, Fanny. Thursday."

Two

Changes

Warm, fat tears drip down my cheeks and onto the piles of Mama's lifeless clothes. Before he left for his trip, Papa ordered me to empty her closet. He said I could keep what I want, and I should bundle up the rest for charity. I'm trying to finish this task before Louie comes home from school.

"Fanny, where are you?" True to her word, Aunt Freda has returned. I close the door firmly and head to the kitchen. My aunt pulls a warm apple cake from her bag.

"Put the kettle on, Fanny. Let's have some tea while we talk." I turn my back and wipe my eyes with a linen napkin. I put Mama's favorite sugar bowl in the middle of the kitchen table. It's white china with blue scrolls. Mama had once admired it, and Cousin Bessie gave it to her before she left for Argentina.

I cut two slices of the moist cake and set each on a small plate. Then, I place a tall silver spoon into each of the thick drinking glasses, and pour in the dark, steamy tea. Aunt Freda takes two sugar cubes and holds them between her teeth as she sips. I warm my hands around my glass, waiting for her to begin.

"Fanny, dear, Uncle Avram is feeling a little better. He and I will be leaving in a few days. His cousin has sent for us. We will stay with Sophie and her husband in New York. It breaks my heart to leave you."

The steam from the tea blurs my vision. I can't see my aunt clearly, but I hear her say, "I'll send for you soon, Fanny, very soon."

"It might be too late."

"Hush, child." She hands me a small purse and a scrap of paper. It looks like the corner of an envelope. I see there is some writing on it. "Here is some money and the address in New York. Keep it hidden for now. Not a word to anyone."

⌒

Papa arrives late Thursday, bearing gifts and some unexpected news. After dinner, he tells me to meet him in his study. Louie helps me to clear the table and then goes to his room to look at his new books.

I pause outside the study door. I can smell Papa's sealing wax. I peek inside. Papa is pressing down on an envelope flap with his special stick. I watch as he removes it with the greatest care and brushes his finger over the thick stamp. Louie told me that the raised part shows the letters in Papa's name. I'm so busy staring at the red bumpy wax, wondering what important message might be inside, that I am startled to hear Papa's voice.

"Come in, Fanny, and sit down."

"Where, Papa?"

I'd only been in this room to bring tea to Papa, or to clean when he wasn't there.

"Here, take my chair, child."

This is not a good sign. I'm worried. Papa doesn't sit. He paces back and forth, gazing out the window at the night sky. The deep blue reminds me of the present he brought for me.

It's a large piece of velvet fabric. Papa said it was for a party dress. We had not been to any celebrations for a long time, and I am wondering which of my cousins will be next to wed.

Papa turns to look at me, sitting in his chair. "Hmm, Fanny, this past year has been hard for all of us, and you, especially, have been an excellent daughter. You'll be a wonderful wife and mother someday."

"Papa..."

"I have arranged a match for you, but not right away. First, you'll have a new mama."

"What?" Papa unlocks the top drawer of his desk and hands me a small pale-blue box. My heart thumps against my chest. I hold my breath.

"I was waiting for your wedding day to give these to you, Fanny. They were my engagement gift to Shira. I want you to wear them next week and then save them for your special day."

Aunt Freda made a beautiful blue velvet dress for me to wear, but she is not here. Uncle Avram's recovery was only temporary. He's weaker than ever, and their move to America will have to wait. I'm sorry to hear about my uncle's illness, but I'm secretly relieved that Aunt Freda will be here a while longer.

There is a small party in honor of Papa's marriage to Mrs. Ida Himoff, also widowed for one year. Now she will be Mrs. Ida Tatch. She is wearing the garnet necklace that Papa bought for her, but she cannot take her eyes off my ears. Mama's ruby earrings are in the shape of teardrops. They are not big, but they seem to catch every bit of light in the room.

The bride's sister is hosting the celebration, and most of the guests are their relatives. We don't have much family left here. Papa's new wife has two married daughters, now living in Canada. She has no other children, but plenty of noisy nieces and nephews. Louie soon tires of their company and comes over to sit with me. "Where's Canada, Louie?"

"It's part of America, north of New York. I'll show you when we get home. One of the books Papa brought me is full of maps." I would like to look at it to see where Aunt Freda will live, but I can't tell Louie about her plans for leaving. That has to remain a secret for now.

"Ouch!" One of the larger nephews shoves Louie off his seat and sits very close to me. I lower my head and move my chair a little.

"Just as they say, a shy girl. Why don't you look up, so I can see what your long eyelashes are hiding?" The heat and color rise quickly from my collarbone up to the top of my head. I'm burning with shame and anger. Where did this creature learn his manners? As I leave to get some air, I hear him tell Louie, "I'm going to marry your sister one day, and then she won't be able to walk away from me."

"She's already been promised."

"But not married yet. Promises can be broken."

⟳

"Mama said to help you with the dishes, Fanny." I stare at Louie.

"I mean...Papa's wife."

"It's OK, Louie, she is your mama now."

The truth is, she's won Louie over, and he has become the son she never had. The study is no longer Papa's bedroom. He's back in his old bed with his new wife. Mama's emptied closet is now stuffed with Ida's clothes. Her ample bottom is filling Mama's forsaken chairs, but she has not taken my place in the kitchen. Ida doesn't like to cook, although she certainly likes to eat.

Another thing she likes to do is spend time in Papa's shop, making sure he doesn't give extra material to the customers. She checks to see that he always gets paid in full. Papa lets her have her way most of the time, but he has put his foot down about her relatives. She can go to visit them, if she wishes, but they cannot come here. Their first argument was about her nephews.

"I don't want those ill-mannered brats running in and out of this house, Ida. The older ones, especially, cannot be near Fanny. She's been promised to a very fine young man, and I don't want rumors spreading about her virtue."

"Don't worry, Chaim, he won't back out. You're handing him a very generous dowry."

"Ida, Sholom is a scholar, refined and well educated. Fanny deserves a good husband. I want that for her, and I promised Shira."

"Shira is gone. I'm here, now, and I should have a say."

"Not about this."

I used to look forward to Thursdays. Louie's school got out early, and he would accompany me to market. Louie always carried the basket, so that I could select the best food, as Mama had taught me to do. All of our purchases were charged to Papa's accounts. We were allowed to stop in the village sweet shop for a treat and to visit with our friends. It was like a weekly holiday.

Now I hate Thursdays. Ida is my marketing companion, and I'm the one who carries the basket. She checks the price on everything and limits what I can buy. There is no stopping for treats or friends.

This Thursday is different. Papa is away on a buying trip, and Ida seems to have her own plans. As soon as Louie gets home from school, she hands him the market basket and practically pushes us out the door. "Take your time, children, and don't forget to stop for a treat."

We're just a few steps away from the house, when I see Ida's sister enter the side door. Hmm. Louie and I stay away a long time but arrive in time to see Mrs. Brodsky leave in a huff. I hear Ida call out to her, "Think about it. I'll make it worth your while."

What is she up to? Is she already making a match for Louie, without Papa? He'll be furious. Maybe she's acting as broker for her oldest nephew. That's not an easy task. Who would want him? From what I hear, he's a lazy student and a bully.

⁓

*I*t's market day again, and I'm waiting for Ida, so we can get started. I'm thinking about what to buy for Papa's welcome-back dinner tomorrow.

"Fanny...I'm ready."

"You're not coming this time. Stay home and finish cleaning. Louie and I will purchase the food."

"What do you mean? Louie doesn't know what I need."

"What's one thing more or less? Do as I say, Fanny."

It seems like Ida and Louie are taking a long time, and they're probably buying all the wrong things. Every once in a while I think I hear them coming, and I look outside. I don't see anyone, so I finish my chores and go to my room to rest.

Strange things seem to be happening. I don't know what they are, but I have a worried feeling. Mama's ruby earrings are in my top drawer, hidden beneath a pile of underwear. I know Ida would love to find them. I hold the little square box in my hand for a moment and then place it in my third drawer, along with the full purse and the papers I've saved. I cover it all with my nightshirts, as I push my concerns about the future away for now.

I can't see Papa when he arrives, a day early, but I do hear him yell out, "What are you doing here? Stay away from this house!"

I hear the door slam and someone running fast. When I ask Papa who he was talking to, he says, "Never mind, Fanny, where is she?" He means his wife.

"She went to the market with Louie."

"With Louie? Did she tell you to stay here by yourself?"

*P*apa and Ida had a big fight when she returned from market with Louie (bringing all the wrong items). The argument was in Papa's study, but I could hear some of the icy words cut through the closed door...*nephew, scoundrel, irresponsible, trust.*

Finally, Ida walked out, head held high, and went straight into her bedroom. She did come to the table for dinner. She spoke to Louie and no one else. Somehow, she seems annoyed with me. I'd like to know what I've done wrong.

I wake up this morning with a heavy weight on my heart. There's a problem, but I don't know what it is. I'm always the first one to rise. I wrap Mama's woolen shawl around my head and shoulders and trudge through the crackling snow to use the outhouse and clean it out for the day.

I try to walk back in my own footsteps to form a path for the others. The well is frozen over, so I collect a large pan full of icicles and snow. I put this on the stove to use for making tea and for washing. After breakfast, I clean up, put the dirty clothes in to soak, and begin to prepare the evening meal. I combine flour, yeast, eggs, and water for the challah. I cover the mixture with a dishtowel and let it rise. I return several times to knead again and again until my arms ache. Finally, I divide the dough into three parts, roll them out, and form a braid. I brush the top with a little of the beaten egg. As the aroma of the baking bread wafts through the kitchen, I start the soup.

The chicken that Ida brought needs plucking. Of course, she wouldn't part with the small change it costs for the butcher to do the job. This is the task I hate the most. Pulling out the tail feathers, especially, cuts right under my fingernails, and scrapes my knuckles. At last, I'm able to put the cleaned chicken into the boiling water, along with the onion, carrots, celery, parsley, and dill. No parsnip? That's what gives the soup a sweeter taste. Ida forgot it. Oh, well.

While the soup simmers, I polish all the furniture in the parlor, rinse out the laundry, and hang the wet clothes on the frozen line outside. I could use an extra set of hands to lift the sodden sheets. They weigh a ton and keep slipping out of my small fists.

The wet laundry has soaked through my apron and housedress, so I head to my room to change clothes. My shivering body yearns to climb back into bed and hide under my feather quilt for the rest of the day. No chance!

My stomach starts to rumble, and I know it's lunchtime. I cut thick slices of the brown bread I made yesterday and prepare three sandwiches with slabs of sharp yellow cheese and butter. I place one on a plate, cover it with a cloth napkin, and leave it on the kitchen table. I put the others in a sack and tap on Ida's door. "Lunch," I say quietly, and head down to Papa's shop.

I can see him at the far end of the counter, talking seriously to one customer. I decide to wait, so we can have lunch together. Finally, the woman turns to leave, calling back to Papa, "Sorry, but you know it's not my fault. I'll see what else I can do." As she walks past me, shaking her head, eyes downcast, I see that this is no ordinary customer.

"What did Mrs. Brodsky want, Papa?"

"Don't worry, Fanny. It will all work out."

I don't know what Papa means, but he doesn't say anything else. After lunch, I go back to the house, clean the lunch dishes, and put the heavy iron on the stove to heat up. I cover the kitchen table with a thick blanket and head outside to bring in the wash.

The iron is bulky and hard to maneuver. I return it to the stove over and over to keep it warm. I need both hands to lift the iron, and I have to be careful not to burn my fingers. Even so, I don't hate this job. I breathe in the steam that rises as the iron hits the icy garments, and I pretend that I'm smoothing my problems away. I always save the Sabbath tablecloth for last. I press it gently and watch as the stiff white linen relaxes. I fold it carefully, running my fingertips over the blue embroidery. I feel Mama's touch in every stitch.

I give the cloth a quick shake, and as it billows above the dining room table, I hear Ida call out to Louie, "Tell your sister to save the chicken wings for me." I catch the tablecloth in midair, fold it up as small as I can, and place it in my third drawer next to my secret stash. I tiptoe out of my room, and reach into the cupboard for another white and blue cloth.

Ida walks in to check on my progress. "Where is the good Sabbath cloth?" *Oh, great, she's talking to me again. I'm ready for her.* "It needs mending." I set the table by myself. Ida, of course, does nothing, and on top of that, she occupies Louie's free time. He used to keep me company while I worked and enjoyed helping out. Now he's often busy reading letters to Ida from her daughters' husbands, and sometimes, stories from his books. She, in turn, offers him sweets and compliments. He seems happy when he's with her. Louie was very young when Mama began to get sick. Manya's away, and I'm so busy. Papa is Papa. He loves us, but he doesn't allow us to get too close. When he arrives at the table, he's freshly scrubbed but not smiling. He blesses the wine and bread and then his children. He does not even glance at his wife.

19

He calls me over to his study after dinner. "I want to tell you myself, Fanny, before gossip reaches you. The marriage arrangement with Sholom is off. His older brother cancelled the deal. I think maybe they're planning to go to America. Don't worry, I'll find a good match for you."

"Please don't hurry."

"It will be fine."

"Good night, Papa."

Sabbath has ended, and so has the peace it brings. After breakfast, Papa pushes his chair back, stands, and looks straight at Ida. "I want to speak with you in the study."

"You can talk to yourself in there, if you wish. This is my home now, and I'll come and go as I please. That reminds me, my sister will be here later for tea. Fanny, be a dear, and bake a nice cake for us. Bluma likes nut cake." Papa opens his mouth, looks around him for some invisible help, and closes it. Then he retreats to his study, alone.

After a while, he emerges with his coat on. "Fanny, make an apple cake for me, and bring it to the shop later."

My hands know the right measurements for each ingredient. First I slice the apples for Papa's cake, sprinkle lemon juice, sugar, and cinnamon on top. Then I add Mama's special touch, a swish of brandy. The flavors blend while I make the batter for the nut cake. I combine flour, sugar, butter, milk, eggs, a teaspoon of vanilla, and a pinch of salt. But somehow, when I reach into the salt jar with my thumb and forefinger, I come out with a fistful. I throw it into the bowl. Too late! I beat the batter hard with the wooden spoon and pour it into the buttered pan. Just before I put it in the oven, I smash the walnuts with the side of a glass and toss the pieces over the batter.

I'm more careful with Papa's cake. I pour this batter into another buttered pan and top it with the moist apple slices, arranged into family groups. Aunt Freda and Uncle Avram are top left, Manya, Jacob, and their baby son, Adam, are top right. I place some of my cousins along the bottom of the cake. Four more slivers represent Papa, Louie, Ida, and me. I put them smack in the middle. I look at the design and I move Ida's slice to the side. Then I change my mind, put Ida back with the group, and take my slice away...for good.

When the baking is done, I leave the nut cake on a platter in the middle of the kitchen table to cool. Let Ida set the table herself.

The apple cake is still bubbling when I open the door to the shop. Mrs. Brodsky is there again, this time talking loudly. "I didn't know Ida would be a troublemaker. She came highly recommended. I can't undo what's happened to Fanny's reputation. Maybe she'll have to settle for the nephew."

"He's a bum."

"He can change. Why don't you give him a chance?"

"Our business is finished. Good-bye."

After she shuts the door loudly behind her I ask, "Papa, what's happening?"

"Oh, Fanny, you know people talk nonsense. This will soon die down. Mmm, delicious cake. Who wouldn't want to marry you?"

When I return home, Ida's sister is gone, but the dirty plates and crumbs still litter the table.

"What happened with the cake? I had told Bluma that you were a great baker, and I was embarrassed."

"I guess a little extra salt fell into the batter, and I couldn't get it out."

"Be more careful next time. You should try to stay on my sister's good side. She'll be your mother-in-law one day."

"Never!"

"Too late, Fanny, it's already in the mix."

The only remnant of the long hard winter is the melting border of snow in the field. I breathe in deeply as I struggle with the wet laundry. I can smell spring in the air, and some hope, too. In my dream, Mama had said that this would be my season.

"Fanny!" I see Ida's head sticking out of the back window. "When you make lunch, pack an extra sandwich and bring it down to the shop."

I mutter, "Louie's in school today, and he has his lunch with him."

"It's not for your brother. Your Papa has a new assistant." The helper, of course, is Ida's worthless nephew.

I arrive at Papa's shop a bit later. "Lunch, Papa," I say, looking straight ahead.

"Leave it on the counter and go upstairs, Fanny." As I turn toward the door, I can feel the boy's beady eyes on my back. Papa calls out to him, "Get back to work, young man, and keep your eyes to yourself."

"Maybe, I will...for now."

I see Papa shrug and take his sandwich to the back of the shop.

Back at home, I find Ida is not in the kitchen. She has already eaten. Her empty plate awaits me. I hear her in my room. I peek in and see her rummaging through my top drawer.

"What are you doing?" I know what she's looking for.

She's startled for only a moment. "Just checking to see if you need underwear. I'll be going to the next town tomorrow on a shopping trip with Bluma and her husband. Next time, you'll come along to get new shoes for your engagement dinner."

"My what?"

"Let's not pretend, Fanny. You know what's meant to happen. Your Papa's plans fell through. You don't need a fancy scholar for a husband. You'll be fine with Reuben. It's a

22

practical match. He'll learn all about the business and help to make it even better. Your Papa isn't getting any younger. Even you can see the change in him. Don't worry, your life won't be very different. Reuben will move in with us after the wedding, and we'll all be together. Everything you need is right here."

"I don't want to get married yet, and certainly not to him."

"Watch your mouth, Fanny. This is not your decision. The engagement will be made official on May 16, but we'll wait one year for the marriage ceremony."

She reaches into my drawer again, counts the undergarments, and shuts it firmly. I feel a tightening in my stomach, and I clench my fists.

Later, that night, as I prepare for bed, I take out a clean nightshirt from my third drawer, and I wonder if I'll ever be able to escape. I remove the Sabbath cloth, the ruby earrings, and the rest of my stash. I glance briefly at the photo of the American classroom, and somehow it doesn't seem so faraway. I stuff it all into a pillowcase and fold it over. I slip the bundle between my quilt and feather bed. There's no chance of Ida discovering my precious package. She does not make beds.

THREE

A Big Decision

Mama always said to be ready when opportunity knocks. It's Aunt Freda's neighbor banging at the kitchen door. "Fanny, come quickly. Your Uncle Avram died early this morning. Poor man. He'd suffered enough. He's at peace now. Your aunt needs you to help out with the shiva and all." She's gone as quickly as she arrived.

After a few minutes, Papa comes downstairs to check on me. He hands me a leather satchel and tells me to pack enough clothing for my week with Freda. I leave the rest of the breakfast dishes in the sink, dry my hands, and rush to my room.

I reach under my quilt, pull out the hidden pillowcase, and use it to line the bottom of the bag. I cover this with seven days worth of clothing.

Aunt Freda's house is on the other side of the village. As I walk across the square with my satchel, people call out to me.

"My sympathies to your aunt."

"Tell Freda I'll be over tomorrow."

"I'm sorry for her loss."

Everyone knows exactly where I'm going and why. There are no secrets in this little town.

"Good, Fanny, you're here." Dora, a neighbor, is already working in the kitchen. "Your aunt says to consult you about everything." She points to a man pacing back and forth at the side door. "He brought the eggs, and now he won't leave. He keeps asking to see Freda."

He is known as Alexius, the deliveryman. He has an old gray horse that pulls the wagon for any merchant in need. I learned a little Russian from helping Papa in his shop.

"How much," I ask. I think he's waiting to be paid.

"No, Miss, Mrs. Freda, please." He waits.

I enter the bedroom quietly. Her eyes are half-closed, but she's not sleeping. I throw my arms around her.

"Auntie, I'm so sorry..."

"Don't worry, Fanny, it was his time."

"I don't want to bother you, but the delivery man, Alexius, insists on seeing you."

"Give me my purse, Fanny, and wait here for me." She takes a coat off the hook and walks out the side door. I look out of the window and see her talking rapidly to the man. She hands him what looks like a lot of coins. He places one finger over his mouth, nods his head solemnly, and leaves.

So much ceremony over eggs.

⌒

Aunt Freda is keeping me close to her. The rabbi rips the collar on my aunt's blouse, and does the same for Uncle Avram's sister. He prays at the gravesite, and the men take turns tossing shovelfuls of earth onto the simple casket.

"Good-bye, Avram," my aunt whispers, and we walk back slowly, arm in arm. Some of the peasants working in the fields nod to us solemnly and remove their hats as we pass

by. My uncle was known to be a kind man and a fair busi-
nessman in both communities. He dealt in gems, large and
small, as well as gold and silver. The Russians often came to
him when they needed christening gifts or wedding rings.
They were always treated with respect.

*J*t's early April, and there's still a chill in the air. The
neighbors are in her house preparing the traditional
funeral meal. The house invites us in with the warmth of
the fireplace and the aromas of brewing coffee and freshly
baked bread. A bowl of boiled eggs sits in the center of the
table. Aunt Freda lights the tall seven-day candle given to
her by the rabbi. She and her sister-in-law, Bertha, sit side
by side on a low bench. Friends and neighbors offer their
condolences and visit for a while. Most people leave well before dark. Since we are forced to live far from cities, there
is always the fear of hungry wolves or wild boars. Papa and
Louie are the last to depart. Bertha sleeps in the guest room,
and I stay with my aunt. She closes the door firmly and pulls
me close to her.

"Listen carefully, Fanny. I've been planning this for quite
a while. I'll be leaving as soon as the shiva is over. I have two
tickets for the train in Kiev, and two passages on the ship to
New York. Come with me. Take your uncle's place, and we'll
start a new chapter in our lives."

My eyes open wide, and my head starts to hurt. What! It's
like when a bright sun appears suddenly on a dark, cloudy
day. It's welcome, but shocking.

"Don't say anything now, Fanny. You have six more days
to think about it. Once we start, there will be no turning
back. It's a big decision, but the world is bigger than Vahivka.
I'm ready, and as I've told you before, you can count on me.
Let's sleep on it for now."

The second day of shiva passes quickly. When the last visitor leaves, Aunt Freda retires to her room and begins to work. She pulls out her old green sack, half-packed with tightly wrapped garments. Her felt sewing kit is on top. It has many pockets for needles, pins, and thread. My aunt unhooks the topaz earrings she always wears and threads a needle. She carefully removes some of the stitches in the sleeves of one of her blouses. Then she sews each of the earrings into the corner of the cuffs. Amazing!

"I'm almost done, Fanny. All of my gems are well hidden and will help us wherever we go."

"*We?* I'm not sure. I want to go, but can I?"

⟵⟶

*T*he rabbi appears on the evening of the fourth day. He gathers together the eight other men in the room, and looks hopefully toward the door. He needs one more to complete the minyan for formal prayers.

Ida bursts in, followed by the tenth man, Reuben. The rabbi beckons to him.

"One moment, Rabbi, I want to introduce my nephew."

Everyone in the room looks up. "Reuben is Fanny's intended. In another year, we'll ask you to bless their marriage."

Aunt Freda stares at me. I lower my head. A tight knot forms in my throat. The more I try not to cry, the harder it grows. The pain radiates to both ears, and I feel like I'm going to explode. Tears well up in my eyes and roll down my burning cheeks. I can taste the salt on my lips. I start to get up. Ida grabs my arm firmly.

"Not so fast, Fanny. Aren't you going to greet us?"

She smiles sweetly and leans over as if to kiss my cheek. Instead, she whispers in my ear. "I expect you home right after the shiva. No dawdling. There are things to be done and plans to be made."

Late that night, I take Mama's ruby earrings from the pillowcase in my satchel and hand them to my aunt. She stitches them artfully into the seams of one of my vests and kisses me goodnight.

On Friday afternoon, Louie comes by to see us. "Fanny, I miss you. Mama, I mean Ida, says you'll be home for lunch on Monday."

"Sit down and eat something, Louie. You look thinner to me."

"I miss your cooking, too."

"How's Papa?"

"He's all right. Reuben has been helping him in the shop and even staying for dinner most nights." I turn toward the stove to ladle some vegetable soup from the pot. I place the bowl, a napkin, and a spoon on the kitchen table, along with two thick slices of brown bread. I sit next to my brother and watch him as he eats. We've been apart for only five days, but I notice some changes in him. The pale skin on his face is still smooth, but I can see the beginning of a wispy blond mustache. His jaw is more angular, and his features better defined. I look into his deep-blue eyes, and he smiles at me.

"Why are you staring at me? I'm not going to disappear. We'll be together in a few days, and you'll get tired of looking at my funny face soon enough." Louie is so sweet. No wonder Ida loves him. Who wouldn't?

"You know I love you, Louie, and Papa, too."

"Of course, we all love each other." The lump begins to form in my throat again. I can't let Louie see me cry. I get up from the table, rinse my hands and face quickly, and dry them with a dish towel. Louie goes into the living room to see our aunt. She hugs him tightly. She can't tell him that this might be the very last time.

29

I awaken to the sound of church bells just outside the village. It's Sunday. This will be the last day for visitors. Bertha will leave after lunch today. It's a one-hour ride, and she wants to be home before sunset. There have been stories about cossacks attacking wagons on the country roads after dark.

Alexius arrives with his horse and cart promptly at two o'clock. He's still dressed in his church clothes. Aunt Freda instructs me to show him Bertha's luggage. He follows me to the side door, picks up the two traveling bags, and positions them under the passenger seat. Alexius looks up expectantly, and I point to the back of the house. He spots my small leather satchel and Aunt Freda's bulging green sack. He places these in the back of his wagon and covers them with a blanket.

Bertha embraces my aunt. "Freda, take care. I will return on Friday to spend the Sabbath with you."

"Thanks, Bertha, see you then, and..." Aunt Freda lowers her voice. "If anything should ever happen to me, you know that this house and everything in it is yours. It was Avram's wish and mine as well."

Bertha smiles. "Nothing is going to happen, Freda. You were a devoted wife to my brother. He's gone now, may he rest in peace, and you still have a lot of life left in you. I'll be back next week." Alexius helps her into her seat, taps his gray horse lightly on the rump, and we wave good-bye.

The house is still and dark. The only light is the seven-day candle flickering low. There is nothing left for us to do. I get into bed, thinking that this will be a restless night for me. I'm about to leave everything I know, to face whatever awaits me. I should be scared, but somehow I feel very calm, almost numb, and I sleep like a baby.

Dawn breaks just as the wick on the mourning candle turns to ash. We eat breakfast in silence. There's nothing to say. We already know the past, and the future has yet to unfold. Aunt Freda finishes eating her toast and gulps down the rest of her sweet tea. She wraps the remaining loaf of bread in a cloth napkin and stuffs it in her pocket.

I watch my aunt's eyes as they survey the room. She walks over to the dining-room bureau and reaches for her candlesticks. They had belonged to her mother, my grandmother Faiga, for whom I am named.

"Here, Fanny, let's take these with us." Aunt Freda has sewn many pockets inside my coat and the cape I wear over it. The candleholders are cold and heavy. They have solid square bases with sharp corners.

Aunt Freda opens the bottom drawer. She pushes aside a bunch of thick white Sabbath candles. I see her pull out a yellow envelope and roll it into a wad of fabric remnants. I remember the conversation I overheard between Mama and Papa.

"What is that?" I say.

"I'll tell you later. Come on. We have to leave!" She shoves the packet inside her coat.

We close the door firmly behind us but do not lock it. Bertha will return on Friday, as promised. She won't find her sister-in-law here, but she will understand when she sees the note left for her.

⌒

Aunt Freda cannot read or write, but she can draw. She sketched a scene on the back of an envelope sent from New York by Sophie's husband, Mendel. It's a picture of a large woman carrying a sack, accompanied by a young lady. Arrows point to a long train and then a huge ship. Bertha will know. She will miss Freda, but she'll pray for our safe journey.

$\mathcal{F}$OUR

THE ESCAPE

$\mathcal{A}$ny neighbor up this early will see us begin the traditional walk around the village to signify the conclusion of shiva. I am thinking about everything and everyone I'm leaving behind. The people I care about most are Papa and Louie, but I can't even say good-bye. Ida has too much influence over them now, and you never know what she might do. It's best just to go and let them find out.

The Russian authorities want all of us to stay where we are. The young men—and even the older ones with families—are often rounded up for military service. If they try to escape and are caught, I hear they are sent to labor camps in Siberia. Someone told Aunt Freda that my original intended, Shalom, and his two brothers left a few weeks ago. No one knows if they ever reached their destination. The older brother's wife and several children live in a nearby village, and they are waiting for news from him.

I'm beginning to perspire under so many layers of clothing. I feel little twinges in my heart as we pass the homes of our neighbors and friends. When we walk by my own house, my heart sinks down to my belly, and my legs fill up with lead.

I see some movement through the kitchen window, and I hear Ida banging the pots and pans, attempting to make breakfast. My heart climbs back up to its normal place, and the lead drains out of my legs. I put one foot in front of the other without looking back.

We should turn around when we reach the synagogue, to complete the circle to Aunt Freda's house. Instead, we walk straight ahead, past the fields and the Ukrainian church. There is a cemetery in the back, and an entry into the forest.

Alexius is waiting there with his horse and wagon. He helps Aunt Freda into the passenger seat. I climb in the back and sit next to our few belongings, which are covered by the blanket.

The old horse shuffles along through the woods and onto the road leading to Kiev.

Aunt Freda's cape rustles as the wagon moves along. All of her official papers are tucked in one of the hidden pockets. I don't understand what they mean, but Uncle Avram's papers are for me, and my aunt will say that I'm her daughter.

"Alexius, this way." Aunt Freda turns her head toward a larger road.

"No, ma'am!" Alexius points in the direction of a wooden sign with letters on it and begins to cough. "Sick," he says. I understand. There has been talk about many people dying in neighboring villages.

Alexius has chosen an alternate path to Kiev. It is dusty and full of bumps and holes. My stomach is doing somersaults, and I feel dizzy. I rest my heavy head against the blanket in the back of the cart, but I don't sleep. I'm thinking about Aunt Freda's instructions.

She said to let her handle everything and to let her do whatever talking is necessary. We're not to speak Yiddish out loud. Some people might hold that against us. My aunt speaks some Russian, and even a little Polish that she learned while helping her husband in his shop.

I lie on my back and look up. The pale yellow sun sits smack in the middle of the sky. This is the time I used to make lunch and bring it to Papa's shop. White cloud pillows follow our wagon. I picture my soft feather bed in the room where I'll never sleep again.

I turn to my right to watch the trees. They nod their branches solemnly. Some blossoms are beginning to appear. *Where will I be when they are weighted down with ripe fruit?*

I shift my body to face the other side of the road. There are many small houses in the distance. Children of all ages are running in the fields. A little blond boy reminds me of Louie when he was small. An older girl takes him by the hand. Tears well up, and before I know it, I am sobbing.

Aunt Freda spins around. She's whispering, but her face is stern. "Fanny, what are you doing? You can't leave part of your heart in Vahivka. You're going to need all of it for our journey, and for whatever follows. I brought some of Uncle Avram's handkerchiefs. Get one out of my sack, and clean your face."

I reach under the blanket and into the green bag. I feel a sharp prick. The point of my aunt's embroidery scissors has stabbed the palm of my hand. I wrap the large white hankie around the open wound and hold it tightly to stop the bleeding. I close my eyes and begin to doze.

I awaken to a hissing sound. "Cossacks!"

That word is clear in either language. I hear the hooves of their horses coming closer. I see a flash of white as they emerge from the woods and enter our road. Alexius tries in vain to speed up. It's too late to hide. They've seen us. If we're lucky, they'll just rob us of our belongings and be on their way.

We need to keep everything we have with us, and we can't trust them not to hurt us. I can see Alexius shaking his head from side to side, like a mouse caught in a trap. Even my aunt's strong shoulders are beginning to droop.

The two white steeds are gaining on us. They are kicking up a storm of dust that rains on my kerchief and cloak. We're doomed. The two riders circle our cart. They narrow their eyes to see what they've caught. I keep my head down.

One of the horsemen stays in front, while the younger one climbs into the back. He sneers when he sees me trying to hide. He grabs the blanket with his huge fingers. His breath is hot on my face. The smell of alcohol and sweat makes me gag. I loosen the handkerchief on my right hand and hold it over my mouth as I cough and spit. Saliva drips down the hankie, leaving a gooey trail of blood on my chin. I wipe it with the soiled cloth. The cut in my hand begins to throb. I bring it to my mouth and begin to tremble.

The cossack watches me in horror. He drops the blanket and shouts out a word that I don't understand. He jumps off the wagon and onto his horse. His companion follows quickly in the direction of the mountains.

Alexius coaxes his horse onto a side road, down a rocky path, and into the woods. We do not look behind us or even listen for the return of our pursuers.

Aunt Freda brings me some water and helps me to wash my face and hands. She removes the loaf of bread from her coat and breaks off three pieces.

"What did he say, Auntie?"

"Consumption!" She bursts out laughing. "The brave cossacks, not afraid of anything except for a clever girl with a cut on her hand." Aunt Freda starts to shake all over, and then her laughter turns to tears. She pulls out another of her husband's hankies and wipes her face. She takes a deep breath and hugs me tight.

We eat our bread and wait until the sun begins to sink down behind the trees. Alexius taps the reins. "Time to go, Luba. You're a good girl. Just a little longer, I promise." Luba's head swivels back and forth, as if to say, "You lied, you lied. It's not a short ride." The moon follows the wagon out of the woods and onto another road. The stars stare at me. Each one poses a question.

Why are you leaving?
Won't you miss your home?
Where will you go?
What will you find there?
Aren't you afraid?
What shall we tell your Papa? and Louie?...and Ida?

"*Stop it.*" I shake my fist at the blinking stars.

"Shah, Fanny, close your eyes."

As I fall into the rhythm of the wagon wheels, I hear Mama's voice in my head. "The wheels turn, life goes on."

And so we go.

⟋

I shade my eyes with my hands. The sun's broad rays beam on large splendid homes, one after another. The city is beginning its day. I see a group of women wrapping themselves in plush Persian lamb coats to ward off the morning chill. Their high buckled shoes tap out a confident beat as they cross the wide cobblestone street.

Gorgeous carriages, pulled by proud white horses, pass us by. Luba lowers her tired head. Alexius tugs at the tattered reins. We pass a huge park, dotted with explosions of color. My aunt pulls out some paper and a pencil from her sack. She sketches some of the most exotic flowers. More ideas for her embroidery.

Alexius points to several large buildings. He says a word that sounds like "school." Oh, yes, even I had heard about Kiev University, a wonderful place to study, unless you're a peasant, like Alexius, or a Jewish girl, like me.

Tall, flaxen-haired young men are entering the bronze ornamented doors, carrying piles of books. Do these students realize how privileged they are? They are the future doctors, lawyers, and leaders of this world. Their world, not mine.

Alexius carries both of our bags in his left hand. His right hand is clutching a sack of coins. He has opened it once already to tip the boy who's watching Luba and the cart. Aunt Freda lengthens her stride to keep up with Alexius. She's dragging me along by my sleeve.

A frosted-glass dome looms over us all. The dark iron structure, which holds the dome in place, reminds me of a giant spider web. We are the insects, stuck temporarily in its space. "Take your eyes off the ceiling and watch your step, Fanny. I don't want to lose you."

At last, we find two empty seats, near the ticket booths. Aunt Freda leans against the curved wooden bench and rests her feet on her green sack. I keep my satchel on my lap and begin to study the station in the same way Louie used to begin a new book.

Alexius walks toward a row of ticket booths, now able to grasp the money sack with both hands. He has our documents inside his jacket pocket. He keeps turning to look at us and then back to stare at the signs ahead of him. As he gets closer to the ticket sellers, I see him pause, take a deep breath, and select one. What's his problem? Those signs must be in his own language. Is it possible he can't read them? Well, at least he can speak to the agent when he pays our fare.

"Here, Fanny, eat this. You're looking pale." My aunt hands me the heel of the bread.

"What about you? Aren't you going to eat something?" The one who looks pale is Aunt Freda.

"As soon as Alexius returns, we'll buy some tea and cake from the vendors. You're a growing girl. I'll eat later." I munch on the dry bread and watch Alexius.

Just then, Aunt Freda calls out and lurches forward. Her head falls into her lap.

"Auntie! What's the matter?"

I try to lift her head, but it keeps flopping back. I grab her arm. It feels cold and damp. "Wake up, Aunt Freda, please don't die! I need you! Wake up!" I'm screaming in Yiddish.

People are looking at me. An older woman in a headscarf walks over. "Shah, maydele. It's OK." She takes a tiny bottle out of her pocket, and shakes it over her hankie. The handkerchief is placed under my aunt's nose and then onto her forehead. Aunt Freda's eyes pop open, and she straightens up.

"What's all the fuss about? I was just dozing."

Why is she saying that? She must know she fainted. One minute, she tells me to be a grown-up, to be strong, and the next, she tries to protect me from the truth, as if I were a little girl. Sometimes I'm not sure which I am, either. The stale breadcrumbs are scratching the back of my throat.

"Fanny, why is Alexius taking so long?" My eyes scan the lines in front of each booth. He's not in any of them. My heart skips a beat. I stand on my tiptoes and then on the bench. I make a full circle. I can see hundreds of people all around, but absolutely no Alexius. No tickets. No coins, no documents. We cannot travel without them. And, suddenly, it hits me. I know for sure. I do not want to go back to Vahivka. I cannot go back to that way of life. I close my eyes. *Help us*, I pray in my head, *please let us go forward.*

The old woman takes my trembling hand in her own. "Be brave, sweet girl, stay strong. You'll get where you're supposed to be—in time." She lifts my chin with her other hand and directs her gaze toward the top of my head. I look straight into her eyes. They are the same shade of gray as Mama's and mine.

Aunt Freda pulls out three coins from one of her pockets. "Here, Fanny, go find a food cart, and buy tea and cake for the three of us. Don't speak to the vendor. Just point out what you want, and don't get lost. Worrying about Alexius is enough for me."

The old woman sits next to Aunt Freda and waves to me. The food carts are on the other side of the station, behind the ticket booths. Each of the vendors is calling out to passers-by, offering wares in a variety of languages and tones. They sound like chirping birds. I choose the cart of the vendor with the softest voice, and I point.

I'm balancing a tray with three steaming mugs and a plate with three slices of dark cake. A red ball rolls between my legs, followed by a small blond boy. The mugs clink against each other, and a burst of the hot liquid splatters my wrist. I wince a little and steady my purchase.

"Fyodor!"

The boy picks up his ball, and walks over to a woman who must be his mother. That is, if she's real. She looks exactly like a grown-up porcelain doll. Her hair is the same color as the honey cake I used to make for holiday dinners. It's piled on top of her head and held in place by a circle of gem-studded combs. I remember that it's rude to stare, so I lower my gaze to the hem of her brown velvet coat and shiny pointed shoes.

After a few steps, I raise my eyes just enough to spot Aunt Freda and her new friend. I place our snack on the bench and sit down. My wrist is beginning to blister. As I reach for my mug, I hear Aunt Freda gasp. I see the porcelain doll again. She pushes her son in front of her. He's still holding his ball. He stares at the floor and mumbles a few syllables. His mother pokes him gently. Fyodor lifts his head just high enough to focus on my scalded wrist.

"Izvinitye."

He looks very sorry. I nod my head. His mother lifts my arm to examine the burn mark. Her hand reminds me of the white satin Papa sells for wedding gowns. Her nails are shaped in perfect ovals and glimmer like pink pearls. I wish I could hide my rough, blotchy hands. The lady wraps a cool hankie around my wrist and hands Aunt Freda a tin box. For once, my aunt has nothing to say. Her mouth remains closed, but her eyes are as big as saucers.

Fyodor and his mama walk away, leaving us to our tea and cake. I remove the handkerchief. It smells like violets and is embroidered with a purple crown and gold letters, matching exactly the crest on the tin box.

Aunt Freda finds her voice. "How do you like that?" she asks the old woman. "I send Fanny to buy tea, and she returns with a countess!"

We are so busy studying our gifts that we don't notice Alexius until he is standing right in front of us, smiling and holding up two train passes and all of our papers. Aunt Freda pockets them, and tells Alexius to sit. She points to the cover of the tin box before lifting it to reveal the most amazing assortment of cookies. Each one is sprinkled with colored sugar in the shape of a crown. So for a brief moment, in the middle of this bustling, noisy, and confusing hub, we relax and have a royal tea party.

After a while, Alexius points to the iron clock high above the ticket booths and then at a large door at the other end of the station.

"Time to go, Fanny."

Aunt Freda hugs the old lady and hands her the tin box, still half-filled with sweet cookies. The woman kisses my cheek. "Go in good health, and pay attention. Life is interesting, you know."

Alexius bows to us. His eyes are moist. He makes the sign of a cross with his right hand, turns away, and is gone.

FIVE

On the Train

"Pick up your step, Fanny. We don't want to miss our train." I've never seen my aunt walk so fast. The tea party seems to have revived her. "And lift your head. You can't spend your life looking at the floor. You'll never get anywhere that way."

Aunt Freda keeps moving. I try to focus my eyes on her skirt, but something shiny catches my eye. It's one of the countess's combs, brown tortoiseshell with yellow stones, forming a crown at the top. I turn around to scan the area for Fyodor or his mama. No sign.

"Fanny!" My aunt is boarding the train. I run right into a giant of a man. He shouts at me and blocks my path. I don't know what to do. The train's shrill whistle pierces my ear. Beads of sweat are dotting my forehead. One drips down to my wrist. "Ouch." The word comes to me. "Izvinitye," I call out and look straight into his angry eyes.

He bursts out laughing, steps aside, and helps me climb the steps.

The entrance to the train is jam-packed with people, all trying to squeeze through the door at once. Someone keeps knocking my satchel against my leg. My boots are scuffed with footprints of all sizes and shapes. I'm trying to locate Aunt Freda. I open my mouth to call her name. The sound of my voice disappears into the gray, smoky air. Chunks of black soot land on my lips and tongue. I try to wipe them off with my sleeve. My feet are no longer moving on their own. I'm being shoved along with the masses. My knees are trembling. For a moment, I feel like sinking down to the floor, covering my head with my hands, and letting everyone step over me.

Then I hear Aunt Freda's voice above the din. "Lift your head, Fanny!" I jut my chin out and raise my eyes just enough to spot a flash of green. I stand on my tiptoes and crane my neck. It's Aunt Freda's sack!

From somewhere with me, a bolt of strength emerges. With all my might, I push and tunnel my way through the crowd, in the direction of the green sack. A strong hand grabs my arm and pulls me to the side. It's my aunt. The sack is still on the top of her head. She takes it down and drags me the rest of the way to the second-class section. I sink into my seat and collapse like the rag doll I left on my bed in Vahivka.

Through half-opened eyes, I see the poorest passengers shuffling down the narrow aisles, heading toward the last car. They are carrying overdressed babies and lugging lifetimes of possessions, rolled into feather beds. The quilts are tied tight with string and long strips of cloth. Pots and pans dangle from the knots. I hope we can get a good soup kettle in America. What I wouldn't do for a large bowl of steaming yellow chicken broth, chock-full of slippery noodles and sliced carrots. For now, the only warmth on my tongue is one salty tear.

A man, followed by an elegant lady and a young girl with her nose buried in a book pushes a huge luggage cart just past my window. As he gets closer, I can see that the elegant lady is none other than the countess. The girl must be Fyodor's sister. She's still reading. So would I, if only I had a book, and if I could read. Back in Vahivka, that was not a possibility, but maybe in America it could happen. The American classroom photo flashes in my mind. I mean, probably it will happen for me there...if I get there...when I get there. I will make it happen, somehow.

I crane my neck to watch the countess, her family, and her luggage enter the second car. "Auntie, look, the countess is on our train. Can you imagine that? Now, I can give her the comb I found."

"Fanny, keep the comb. I'm sure she has no need for it."

"But it's not mine."

"That's true, but I think you're meant to have it. A royal family will have a private car. The guard won't let you in. Just stay with me, and forget about the countess and her comb." I try.

I close my eyes and let myself fall into the click-clack rhythm beneath my seat. I'm not sleeping, but I hear someone snoring. It's my aunt, succumbing to the beat of the train. Her head rests on her green sack. I touch the outside of my jacket pocket and feel the outline of the comb. I hold my breath, tiptoe past Aunt Freda, and start down the aisle.

The guard's uniform is dark blue with gold braiding on the shoulders and matching buttons down the front of his jacket. A navy hat with a gold brim fits tightly on his bulbous head. His cheeks are round and pink, and except for the fancy uniform, he reminds me of any peasant working in the fields outside of Vahivka.

He lowers his gaze slightly and regards me the way a cat would, ready to pounce on a passing mouse. I'm not a mouse, and I need to see the countess. I straighten my spine and pull myself up by raising my shoulders and lengthening my neck. I tilt my chin in the direction of the gold-buttoned chest. "Fyodor," I say.

The huge guard continues to stare at me. I suppose he's wondering what on earth I have to do with the countess. I can't see anything, but I do hear movement inside the private car. I hear Fyodor's ball bouncing off the walls, the sound of a table being set, the clinking of glasses, and the clanging of heavy silverware.

I finger the comb again, and I look up at the man who is blocking my entry. His eyes skim over my entire body, stopping momentarily at my chest and hips. Then he swivels his head from side to side. He raises one beefy arm in the air and takes a step toward me. Maybe he's going to hit me. I try to move away, and he shoves me into the corner. I turn my head toward the wall. I don't want any marks on my face. He's not hitting me. His coarse fingers are fumbling with the buttons on my jacket. His other hand reaches under my skirts, pulling my stockings. The more I try to push him away, the more his hands grope me.

I cough hard and spit out the phlegm that is gagging my voice. I spit again and scream with all my might, *"Nyet!"*

There is complete silence for a split second, and then Fyodor's ball hits the door. I scream his name. The door slides open, and out comes the countess herself. The monster in uniform removes his hands and staggers away from me. He attempts to straighten his jacket. He wipes the sweat from his forehead with his sleeve and adjusts his cap. My heart is pounding so hard that I can't hear the countess, but I see her mouth moving fast.

Fyodor smiles and takes my hand. He pulls me into their car. I know it's only a wagon attached to a train, but it looks more like a long, narrow, splendid home. Crystal lights hang from golden hooks above each window. A round table is covered with a beige linen cloth, and set with dainty flowered dishes. The seats are roomy and upholstered with plush purple velvet. There is a gold brocade sofa at the rear of the car.

Fyodor's sister is perched at one end. She is leaning back, resting her blond curls on a large purple cushion. I wonder if her eyes are violet, as well. They are still hidden behind her book. She doesn't lift her head until the countess enters. The girl looks a lot like her mother, but without the smile. Her lips form a straight line of disapproval. Her eyes are blue, like her mama's, but a paler shade.

"*Chai*," says the countess. She puts her arm around my shoulders and walks me over to one of the soft chairs. I still feel shaky, but relieved to have been rescued from the horrible guard. I don't want to think about that at all. I focus on the comb. I take it from my pocket and hand it to the countess. Her eyes open wide—they're more like blue velvet—and then she opens her mouth. Her laughter sounds like tinkling bells. She slips the comb into her honey hair and beckons her children to the table. "Yelena, Fyodor!"

The boy comes running, but the girl remains where she is. She pushes her legs under the sofa cushion, tosses her curls, and hides her icy-blue eyes behind her book. The countess shrugs her shoulders and turns her back to the sullen daughter. Red blotches appear on her forehead and cheeks. A young woman in a black dress and white apron walks over. She dips one of the linen napkins into a glass of ice water, and hands it to her mistress. The countess pats her face and neck with the cloth and lays it down on the table.

Steaming, amber-colored tea is poured into two of the porcelain cups. Fyodor's cup is thicker, with a handle on each side. Instead of painted flowers, pictures of dancing bears encircle the rim. It is half-full of tea and topped with a thick layer of whipped cream. I look around for sugar cubes. There are none to be seen, so I guess I'll have to drink bitter tea; that is, if I can manage the fragile cup. I'm used to drinking tea from a sturdy glass. There will be a lot of new things for me to learn.

The maid lifts the cover of a silver bowl, inserts a small spoon, and scoops up a white powder. She sprinkles it in our teacups. The cascading granules remind me of the first snow that falls each year in Vahivka. Next year's snow will arrive without me. Others will track through its crunchy path to use the outhouse. My feet will be taking a different route. A new one. I close my eyes. The memory of a white blanket of snow turns into a white page in a new book. It will be up to me to learn to write on it. It will be my future.

The countess leans toward me and stirs my tea. I watch her lift her cup with the crook of one finger. She brings it to her lips and sips slowly. Fyodor picks up his mug with both hands and slurps his creamy tea. We eat small triangle-shaped sandwiches. They are made from soft white bread, filled with chopped egg, butter, and greens. They melt in my mouth. I am embarrassed to eat so many, but the countess keeps putting more on my plate.

I'm beginning to worry about my aunt. I push back my chair and rise. "Tante Freda," I say and point toward the door. The countess nods her head. She speaks softly to the maid, who covers the remaining sandwiches with a beige napkin. The young woman carries the sandwich tray in one hand and a gold-colored card with purple writing in the other. She stands next to me. Fyodor runs over and gives me his copybook and a large pencil. He waves good-bye. His mother offers me a thick, glossy magazine. "Freda," she says. Mama always told me to accept gifts graciously. I smile sweetly. The countess glances at her daughter. Yelena has not yet risen from under her book. Maybe I'll be like that one day. No. When I learn to read, I will be the first to share that good fortune with everyone. One day.

I can feel the train slowing down, and I hear a thud just outside. As the door slides open, I feel a chill run down my spine, and my knees begin to buckle. I had forgotten about the horrible guard until now. The countess's servant is just in front, but how will a little maid protect me? The guard approaches. "Verochka." The girl steadies the sandwich tray and lowers her eyelids. I can see the color rising in her cheeks. This is a different man. He appears to be younger and much kinder. He tips his hat in my direction.

"Boris?" asks the maid.

The new guard points to the road on one side of the tracks. I catch a glimpse of my attacker, head down, hatless, and alone. He's fading into the distance, fading away like the memory of a bad dream once the sun emerges.

The countess's gold card helps us to pass through each car without an explanation. My aunt is standing in the aisle next to our seats. She opens her mouth wide when she spots me and closes it again at the sight of my companion. Aunt Freda stares at the two of us. She resumes her seat, shaking her head. The maid places the sandwich tray in my aunt's lap, bows slightly, and begins retracing her steps.

"Well, well, Fanny. Everyone in Vahivka thought you were the quiet one in our family. Some people worried that you were too timid. They should see you now. I guess you're beginning to spread your wings. Save that for the future. Stay close to me from now on. We're going to need each other. You gave me quite a scare. I'm so angry, I don't even want to talk with you right now."

My aunt turns her head toward the window, but not for long. "Was the countess happy to get her comb back?" My aunt lifts the linen napkin and smiles.

"So, another tea party. Tell me all about it." She leans back and enjoys the luscious little sandwiches, while I recount every glittering detail. I describe the décor, the setting, and even the flowered teacups. I tell Aunt Freda about the countess's dismal daughter and her books. I leave out the part about my encounter with Boris.

"You describe everything so well, Fanny, just like your mama. Your stories could fill a book." Aunt Freda shrugs.

"Maybe they will," I say. "And speaking of books, I have another surprise."

I show the copybook and pencil to my aunt.

"These were Fyodor's. Can you believe he gave them to me? He's so sweet, just like Louie."

Aunt Freda nods her head.

"And, that's not all, Auntie. The countess sent something just for you."

I hand her the glossy journal.

"For me, really? Why?"

"Maybe the countess knows you like to sew." My aunt takes an embroidered hankie out of her jacket pocket. She wipes her eyes and brushes some crumbs off her skirt. She adjusts her seating position. And very carefully, she opens her new magazine.

The first page has several sketches of what must be the latest fashions, and many words. The letters are differently shaped than those I've seen before. They seem to be made up of lines and circles. Aunt Freda is focusing her gaze on the black-and-white drawings of ladies modeling puffed-sleeve blouses, flowing party dresses, and lace-trimmed capes.

I open my copybook to a clean page. I hold the thick pencil the way that Louie used to hold his to practice his writing. I make a row of circles, then one of lines. I continue until I reach the bottom. The pencil feels comfortable between my fingers, just as if I'd been writing for years. Until a few weeks ago, my hands had been struggling with heavy pots and pans, large ladles, and a clumsy iron. Those were things I had to do. This will be a different kind of experience. "Everything in time," Mama used to say. *Yes, in time,* I say to myself. But I want the time to go quickly. I want to start my new life. I'm tired of traveling, and we haven't even gotten to the ship. I write page after page, until darkness forces me to close the copybook.

A porter adjusts the oil lamps until they shed a dim light over the dozing passengers. My aunt removes her woolen cape and spreads it out to cover the two of us. I drift in and out of a shallow sleep. My dreams involve circles and lines chasing each other across a barren field. "Hurry," they call to one another, "hurry, or we'll miss the boat."

"Wake up, Fanny, get ready. We have to find our ship." I rub my eyes open and look out of the window. The huge platform is full of movement, mostly in one direction. Pretty soon, we're on the same path. My aunt totes her green sack, and I clutch my leather satchel. We're able to pass people who are struggling with more cumbersome loads.

The dock is almost as wide as the ocean beyond. The sea seems to go on forever. Salty droplets dance on my cheeks and tongue. The dark-green water is streaked with foamy waves. The yellow sun blazes in the blue sky. My clothes are beginning to weigh me down. I feel like shedding some of the layers and flying around like the large gray-and-white birds that live here.

"They're called seagulls," my aunt informs me.

Vendors push carts laden with spicy-smelling meat sandwiches, cakes, and beverages. They are calling out in a language that is familiar to me. "They're speaking German," my aunt tells me. "We're in Germany." She walks over to a wagon and buys a bag of plump braided rolls. "For later. We don't want to miss our ship."

Aunt Freda shows the two tickets to the pretzel seller. He points to the far end of the pier. Two tremendous vessels dominate that area. Crowds of people are lining up, waiting to board. My aunt stares at the letters on the sides of both ships. She looks hard at the words printed on our tickets.

"Aha, Fanny, this is the one." She pulls me over to the left. "Here we go. Stand up straight. These are for the second cabin. No steerage for us."

Most of the people are headed down a shaky staircase, dragging bundles and babies along. Horns are blasting. Smoke is billowing out from tall stacks. My heart is beating wildly.

The ticket collector takes one look at our passes and hands them back to my aunt. She offers them again.

"Nein!" Streams of German words follow. I catch some of them. It sounds like he's calling her a foolish cow who can't even read a simple sign. He screams louder, "SS *Bremen*," and points to the name on the neighboring ship.

For a split second, the world stops. Everyone is looking at us. First my aunt's cheeks redden with shame. Then the color drains out, and she's as pale as a ghost. Her shoulders droop, and head lowered, she follows me down the plank and over to the right.

The SS *Bremen* is twice as large as the wrong ship. It looks as if it could open up and swallow the entire town of Vahivka. I'm straining my neck, trying to see the top of the smoke stacks and hold on to my aunt at the same time. I almost fall over a huge coil of rusty chains. So much for looking up.

I lower my gaze. The dock is littered with huge, tattered ropes and leaking oilcans. The floor is slippery. I lift my skirt and tighten my grip on Aunt Freda's arm. The ship's gangplank is made of splintered wooden beams. It shakes and sways back and forth. Something inside my stomach is doing somersaults. I'm feeling dizzy, but it's my turn to be strong.

S I X

$\mathcal{I}$ try to move forward, but we're stuck smack in the middle of a huge assortment of travelers. They come in all sizes, shapes, and shades. Their words are as varied as their looks. What we all seem to have in common are the layers of clothing we carry on our bodies and faces that reveal exhaustion, fear, and hope all at once. Everyone is trying to board the ship at the same time, causing a bottleneck. A burly man pushes Aunt Freda into my ribs. Her feet slip on the greasy ramp, and the tickets slide out of her hand. I place my satchel on the ground, and put the green sack on top. I seat my aunt quickly and reach down to retrieve our passes. I try to wipe off the smudges with my hankie. I fold them in half and stuff them in my outside pocket.

Aunt Freda and I are pushed along until we reach the ticket collector. He looks almost as weary as his customers. He glances at the soiled papers and points to a steep, descending staircase. It seems as if hundreds of people, with thousands of bundles, are heading down those rickety steps. I think I spot Malka carrying her little brother, but when I look again, all I see is a mass of weary men, women, and children. My aunt shakes her head and holds two fingers in front of the agent's face. He takes another look and points to a long hallway.

At the end of the passage is a large white sign with seven lines of letters, some of which I've seen before, but none that I can read. Below the list of words is an outline drawing of a woman, so I guess the words all say "woman," or something like that, in a variety of languages. I wonder which women here have learned to read and where they come from. I look at the words again and make believe I can read.

A sturdy woman approaches. Her hair is a reddish-brown color and is pulled back in a tight bun. She holds a clipboard in her hands. She stares down at us. My aunt holds out the stained tickets. The clipboard lady says something quickly. I guess she's speaking German. It sounds like "come with me." No smile at all. Her thick ankles bulge out over her tightly laced flat shoes.

The woman makes a sharp right turn, and we follow. There are dozens of doors in this corridor, all painted dark blue. Each one has two black letters on it. She stops at one door halfway down and pushes it open with her elbow. Without another word, she turns her head, and marches back down the hall.

Our room is not much larger than the outhouse in back of the home I left in Vahivka. It is almost as plain. Two narrow beds, one over the other, line the left wall. Each bed has one flat pillow and a green wool blanket. The right wall has a metal chest of drawers. There is one straight-backed chair in between the beds and the dresser. Aunt Freda drops her satchel on the chair, sheds several layers of clothing, and lowers her body onto the bottom bed.

"Fanny, climb onto the top bunk, and we'll both rest for a few minutes. It's been a long day."

I look up and shake my head. "I'm not tired."

"Just a short nap." She glances around the tiny cabin. "Pull the chair close to the beds, and lift yourself up. Later, we'll have a look around. I don't want you wandering off by yourself." Her head plops onto the pillow. Her breathing deepens and quiets to a gentle purr. I cover her with my own cape, straighten my skirt, and set out to find a washroom.

I close the door quietly and study the symbols on the front. They look like this: BR. I stand still for a while, deciding which way to go. When I walked in Vahivka, I knew every turn. The path to the right of our home led to the market. The left-hand road was the one we took to go to the synagogue and Louie's school. Now, I'm lost.

Mama always said that lost things can be found. So I'll try to find myself again. First, I need to wash up. There are signs on every wall, with arrows pointing in different directions. So many words, all a mystery to me. I see the matron again, shepherding another flock of women and girls. I clear my throat. She gives me a hard look. "*Vasser*," I whisper, rubbing my hands together and bringing them to my cheeks. The woman spurts out a few German words, points to a sign, and shakes her head. I begin walking the way the arrow points, taking each step as if treading on eggshells. I pass a door, painted white, with lots of printing on the front. I focus on the strange letters until the door opens from inside. A large woman emerges. She's wearing a shirtwaist dress made of a shiny pink material. A vertical line of brass buttons is closed up to the collar.

This matron is different from the first. As soon as she sees me, a smile appears on her broad face. She takes my hand and leads me over to a large washbasin. The lady hands me a stiff white towel and a small square of soap.

The washroom is clean and warm. The woman in the pink dress is helping some other travelers. She sees that I'm ready to leave and gives me another smile. Tears spring into my eyes. I don't know why. Maybe it's because I've been away from home and familiar faces for so long that a smile, even from a stranger, feels good. The lady opens the white door and points to herself with one finger. "Helga," she says.

"Helga," I repeat. She looks to be about Aunt Freda's age and size.

"Fanny," I say, pointing to myself.

"*Gut*, Fanny." Helga shakes my hand vigorously.

I'm in a hurry to return to our room. If she awakens, and I'm not there, my aunt will be worried. I walk past a corridor filled with blue doors. I study the letters on each of them. RP, SH, GC, and on and on. Oh, at last, RB. I open the door quietly, so as not to startle my aunt. The room looks the same, except for three things: no green sack, no leather satchel, and no Aunt Freda. My legs feel weak. I sit down on the straight metal chair and hold my aching head in both hands.

"Nein!" It's the clipboard lady with two older women, waiting at the open door. I stand up as the new passengers enter. The matron beckons to me, and I follow her down another hallway until we reach the correct door. She points to the letters, BR, calls me a *dummkopf*, and walks away, mumbling to herself.

Aunt Freda is still lying in the bottom bunk, poking the bed above her with the heel of her boot, and calling out, "Fanny, wake up. You've slept enough for now." I begin to giggle. My aunt sees me and laughs, too. For some reason, we can't seem to stop. We laugh until tears roll down our cheeks. My belly starts to hurt. I think I'm hungry. Aunt Freda looks into her sack and finds the bag of pretzels she had bought on the dock. They're a little stale by now, and salty. I'm thirsty. I wonder where we can get something to drink. What about dinner?

There are signs all over the ship. Maybe they answer these questions. Who can help us? "Come on, Fanny, let's have a look around. Stay with me." Fyodor's notebook and pencil are on top of my satchel. I take them with me. We close the door behind us, and I copy down our room letters on a clean page. I write slowly and carefully: BR. That is, B on the left and R on the right.

Helga welcomes us into the washroom. She introduces herself to Aunt Freda and gives her extra soap and towels. Later, she leads us to a large room nearby. It has a very long wooden table. There are many chairs all around it. Three ladies are sitting at one end of the board.

A woman enters from another door. She's wearing a long black dress and white pinafore. She carries a silver tray, laden with three steaming mugs. Each of the tall cups is decorated with a painting of our ship. Helga motions to the server. The woman walks over to where we are standing. "Fanny, Freda, *das iz* Herta." Helga speaks quickly to her friend, waves to us, and leaves.

Herta serves the ladies, bows slightly, and walks the length of the table to the opposite side of the dining room. She pulls out two chairs, and motions to us. Once we are seated, she holds up the palm of her right hand, as if to say, *wait*. Her left hand holds the empty silver tray. Herta pushes the side door open with her hip and backs into what must be some sort of a kitchen.

I start to fidget in my chair. "Auntie, when...?"

"Shah."

Her gaze is focused on the tea drinkers. I take a better look at them. All three have thin faces, tight lips, and straight narrow noses. Maybe they're sisters. They are neatly dressed. Each one is wearing a simple blouse, one blue, one tan, and the other light green. The wide cuffs sport round wooden buttons. The high collars are made of stiff white cotton. The sisters' hairdos are the same. The color is dark brown, with dashes of gray. The hair is pulled back and held up on top of their heads with tortoiseshell combs, not gem-studded ones like the countess has. At least they do not cover their heads with rough woolen scarves like so many of women who boarded the ship with us. These three look like a matched set. I wonder where they come from and why they left. Did they leave anyone behind, like we did? Where are they headed, and what awaits them? Will they always be together? I find myself wondering about other people's futures instead of my own. I'm not ready to think about that yet. "The wheel turns," Mama used to say. There's a lot of turning ahead, I'm sure.

For now, the ladies are busy chatting with each other in their language. They don't seem to notice or acknowledge us at all...that is, until Herta arrives with her tray. This time, there are two steaming ship mugs, and something more. There is an oval platter laden with an assortment of small sandwiches and cookies. The goodies are placed in front of us, and without glancing at the other passengers, Herta retreats.

The women look up from their almost empty cups and stare at us openmouthed. Now it is our turn to ignore them. We are so busy drinking the soothing tea and enjoying our snack, we don't even see them leave.

When Herta returns, she finds an almost empty plate. Only the few sandwiches containing meat remain untouched. Aunt Freda decided that we should try to eat everything offered on our journey in order to stay strong. Everything except meat. We cannot be sure about that.

"*Danke*." My aunt smiles warmly at our benefactor.

Suddenly, a loud whistle blows, followed by a series of horn blasts. Herta leaves everything on the table and rushes out of the room.

The dining-room door opens onto a stream of passengers, all women in this section. We fall into the line. At the end of the hallway, the group expands to include men, and then families, all of us flowing toward the blasting sounds and the wide-open deck.

The large space is filling up quickly. Our fellow travelers are arriving in droves, pushing us forward, until we can move no more. I'm pressed against the cold railing. I look behind me and then all around. I notice that, somehow, this huge crowd has formed sections.

To the left, I see a smaller group of smartly dressed ladies and men. Some are seated on padded, wooden lounges, gazing at the shoreline through long tubes. The people on my right, still coming up the stairs from steerage, are the greatest in number. I try to spot Malka, or anyone else I've seen before. "Look ahead, Fanny. We're leaving."

I can feel the ship—our ship, lurching, moving, and backing farther and farther away from the land, and from those still on it. The dock workers and others are getting smaller as we continue to push away. Many are waving their arms, hats, and scarves in our direction. Most of our shipmates are waving back. Someone's blue handkerchief flies above our heads and over the rail. It lands on the dark, murky water, floats for a moment, and sinks.

A woman behind us screams out. I turn around. It's the sister with the blue blouse. She's crying. Her two companions are trying to console her, offering their own colored hankies. My aunt recognizes the ladies from the dining room. She retrieves a neatly folded handkerchief from the side pocket of her skirt. It is white linen, beautifully embroidered with blue and yellow spring flowers.

Aunt Freda hands it to the blue sister, who stares first at the lovely hankie, and then at my aunt. She shakes her head and tries to return the gift. Aunt Freda pushes it back gently and nods her head vigorously. I can see the lady admiring the careful stitches. "Danke," she whispers, and then she is lost to us as the crowd thickens and swallows us up.

I can no longer see the ocean or the shore. People surround me. I can feel my aunt's hand grasping mine. Booming, screeching sounds become louder and louder as the floor beneath our feet pulls us out to sea. I can hear the thick, heavy waves wallop the sides of the SS *Bremen*. Wavelets of excitement and fear dance within me and finally subside.

Little by little, the crowd thins. People are returning to their quarters. Many descend the stairs. Others file down long corridors, which branch out into narrow hallways. Aunt Freda and I follow the line of women.

Fyodor's copybook is open to our room's letters. I double-check when we get to the entry. I do not want to make the same mistake twice. The door opens into our little room, containing one green sack and one leather satchel. I consider this to be my first reading success. Everyone has to begin somewhere, don't they?

I sit down on the metal chair and hold the pencil between my thumb and third finger. I trace over the BR in my notebook and then draw the outline of a door around them. Next to the door, I make a star. *Good work*, I say to myself. I am my own teacher, for now.

I remove my traveling clothes and place them on top of the dresser. I put on my nightgown, climb onto the thin mattress, and close my eyes.

"What about dinner, Fanny?"

"Tomorrow, Auntie, I'm so sleepy."

I am rocked to sleep by the motion of our ship moving over the sea. I fall deeper and deeper into dreamland, as my body recalls other rhythms of our journey. It remembers the slow steps of our farewell walk around Vahivka, the bumpy ride in Alexius's rickety wagon and the steady click-clack of the train leaving Kiev. And then, it rests.

I don't have any idea what time it is, or if it's morning yet, but my stomach is rumbling. My aunt is dressed and ready for our first full day at sea. She is seated on our one chair. She is not looking at me. Her eyes are darting back and forth between the sketches she made of the gardens we passed in Kiev and the white linen square in her left hand. Her right hand holds a long silver needle, which slides in and out effortlessly, producing a burst of blooms. I clear my throat.

"Finally. Let's get started. I'm hungry."

I now know the way to the washroom and dining room. Both are very busy. We can hardly find a place to sit at the table. The sisters are in the same seats as they were for tea, yesterday. Today, they are all dressed in varying shades of gray. Now I don't know who's who. Oh, yes, one of them is waving her new handkerchief.

We find two chairs near those ladies. They nod to us and resume their conversation. I think they're speaking German. I catch a few words, here and there. Actually, the one word I hear from all sides of the room sounds like *storm*.

Herta appears with a young helper. They begin serving at the far side of the room. As they get closer, I can see that the girl's tray has many identical plates, each containing blobs of loosely scrambled eggs, toasted bread, and slabs of fat-streaked meat. She carelessly plops them down in front of each woman.

Herta's tray holds a variety of offerings. She serves them to certain passengers. Two older ladies are given large bowls filled with steaming oatmeal. Several women receive puffy pastries topped with honey and nuts. Our breakfasts consist of two boiled eggs, a basket of soft rolls, and cherry preserves. I'm happy. I think it's good to be one of Herta's chosen guests. I don't know why it is so, but I'm hoping to stay that way. I finish my meal in record time and place my napkin on the table. Herta picks it up and uses it to wrap up the rest of our rolls. She hands the little package to my aunt and mentions something about a storm.

I feel the ship beginning to sway. Some of the water glasses are clinking against each other. The hurricane lamps are flickering. Herta's helper is running around, collecting whatever remains on the table. Her orange pigtails are bobbing up, down, and sideways. I cover my mouth to hide a giggle. I don't want to hurt her feelings. I know how it is to work hard when you're not quite grown.

My aunt wants to go right back to our quarters. I want to go out on deck.

"Tomorrow is another day, Fanny. Come on, I'll teach you some new stitches."

She thinks sewing is fun. I never liked it. "Just for a minute. Let's see what's happening outside."

Aunt Freda follows reluctantly and waits inside the last door. Why is everyone so nervous? I remember the storms in Vahivka as happy times for me. They brought us all together. As soon as she'd hear the wind whipping through the trees, Mama would call down to Papa's store, "Chaim, *der shturem.*" Then, Manya and I would run outside to help Mama bring in the wash and fetch water. Louie tried to help Papa shutter the windows and latch the doors. By the time the thunder began to clap and lightning bolted across the somber sky, we'd be sitting around the kitchen table. Mama always made pancakes for our storm meals. Their buttery tops glistened in the candlelight. With our bellies full, we'd listen to Papa's Bible stories and Mama's tales of faraway and long ago.

The sharp air brings me back to the here and now. We've just finished breakfast, but the sky is almost as black as night. I can't see the ocean at all, but I can hear it roar. Waves are lashing water onto the deck. The ship's workers are busy climbing up poles, pulling down flags, and clearing the area of all moveable objects.

I wrap my shawl around my head and shoulders and breathe in deeply. I stare up at the angry heavens. "Mama, can you see where I am? What do you think?" I whisper. A gush of wind pushes me hard, and I slide onto the soggy floor. A passing sailor pulls me up and points to a sign posted near the door. "*Verboten,*" he yells. I stare at the bright red letters. That's what they must say. Oh, "*forboten.*" I'm not supposed to be out here.

"Had enough, Fanny?" My aunt just shakes her head. There's nothing more to say. The hallways are quiet. People have already hidden themselves away for the duration. Probably a good idea.

By the time we reach our cabin, I'm beginning to regret my hearty breakfast. My belly is tilting in rhythm with the ship. Something is blocking our door from the inside. I look through the crack. It's a mattress. We maneuver it bit by bit, until we can enter. Things are not as they were. Some clothes are scattered around the small room. The dresser is on its side, and the chair is on top of it. I help my aunt to fix the mess, but it's not easy. There are forces working against us. Every time we put something in its place, it's thrown to another corner of the room, and we have to get out of the way. Maybe, one day, I'll remember this scene and have a good laugh.

Right now, I'm frustrated, a little scared, and very nauseated. We turn the dresser face down. We push it against the door and shove the back of the chair under the chest. Even though it's early, we put on our nightgowns. We deposit our clothing into our carrying cases and hide those under the lower bunk. The bed frames are shaking. We grab my mattress and place it on top of my aunt's bed. We get into the lower bunk, cover ourselves with both blankets, and wait.

I can feel the rolls and jam rising in my gut. I swallow, trying to keep them down. I breathe in slowly then more deeply. The mass in my stomach begins to recede and then jumps up into the back of my throat. I clamp my lips together. My throat is burning. Pressure is building between my ears. The ship jumps again and jerks my mouth open. I choke up some saliva, and hang my head over the side of the bed. I start to gag again. I'm breaking out in a cold sweat. I can feel the room trembling. Or is it just me?

"Come, Fanny, put your head on the pillow." My aunt wipes my brow with her ever-ready hankie. "Try to rest. No sewing for us today."

"I'll be all right."

"Just lie back, and let me tell you a story. We haven't had a chance for a good talk in a long time. We had been apart for a while. I've been wanting to tell you something."

My head is starting to ache. "What is it?"

"Relax, Fanny. Just listen. It's important to me that you know this. You're growing up nicely, Fanny. I'm glad you're not going to get stuck with that oaf, Reuben. You deserve better than that. People always said that you are a lot like your mama, and in many ways that's true. But, somehow, you remind me of myself at your age."

"What do you mean?"

"You have dreams, Fanny. I can see that. So did I. Shira was content to cook with our mama and listen to her stories. For me, the kitchen was never big enough. I wished I could travel with my papa. He was a peddler, always on the road, going from town to town, buying and selling all kinds of items. That's how he met Avram. But that part of the story comes later."

"Did you ask him to take you along?"

"He took my brother, instead. He told me to help out at home. I was much better at needlework than at cooking and baking. On nice days, I sat outdoors with the sewing basket. When I finished the mending, I'd make blouses, aprons, and even tablecloths. I always asked Papa to bring silk threads for my embroidery. One day, he surprised me with an envelope of colored pencils and paper, so I could sketch my designs."

"So that's how you started. You taught yourself."

"I did, but I wished I could learn more. When the paper started running low, I asked Papa for another pack. He told me to pay more attention to housework, and to apply my needle skills for my wedding trunk. I told him I did not want to get married. I wanted to see the world and create art. See what I mean, Fanny? We're not so different."

"But you did get married."

"Not so fast. There's more to tell. My papa reminded me that the eldest daughter must marry before the others. He told me to put my pipe dreams away. So I did, for a while. I tried to cook and help at home, and I started going to market every Thursday to buy food for the Sabbath."

"Just like I did."

"Right, Fanny, and each week, I made the same purchases and saw the same people. I liked the chance to get away from the kitchen. Papa indulged me and gave me a few extra coins to buy some treats. He told me to enjoy these outings, because before long, I'd be keeping house for a nice young husband. I told him to take his time."

"That's just what I told my papa."

"But things changed for you when Ida became your stepmother, and things changed for me, too, in ways I never could have predicted."

"Did something happen in the family?"

"No, it was at the marketplace. Let's see. One Thursday, I noticed a new booth, located a little apart from the other vendors. Something drew me to it like the pull of a magnet. I couldn't resist."

My aunt turns her head toward the wall. When she faces me again, I can see tears welling up in her eyes. She pats them dry with her sleeve.

"As I got closer to the booth, I could see what drew me there. There were tables displaying art supplies, rainbows of paints, pencils, and paper for sale. I was so enchanted with the array of items that, at first, I didn't even notice the artist."

"Really? An artist at the market? What did he look like?"

"Head down, Fanny, the storm is getting worse."

I can hear the most horrible commotion coming from another part of the ship. Crashing, shattering, banging, booming, screeching noises surround us. They seem to go on forever. At last, I peek out from under the pillow. The only sound now is a gentle rumbling. A sigh escapes from deep within me. My brow relaxes. "Auntie, tell me more."

"This is the hard part, Fanny. I never told this to anyone. Your mama knew a little, but we never really talked about it. Everything happened so fast."

"Did you know the artist?" My aunt swallows hard and bites her lower lip.

"No, I'd never seen him before, or anyone like him."

"So, he wasn't from Vahivka, or even Podolia Gubernia?"

"Not at all. Of course, I didn't look at him directly, just out of the corner of my eye. I was not shy. It was because of the way all of us were raised. A young woman could never socialize with a man from outside of the family. It wasn't proper. You know, Fanny, everything was a *shande*. You wouldn't want to bring shame to your family and ruin the chance of a respectable match."

"Things haven't changed much."

"The first time I saw him, he was seated at a large easel, paintbrush in hand. There were other curious shoppers looking at his wares, and also at his painting. I didn't get any closer, but I did sneak a few more looks at him. The third time I did that, he looked up from his work and caught my eye. He smiled right at me, and I turned away. You know, Shira was the beautiful sister. I never even thought I was pretty. But maybe I was." Color rises in my aunt's cheeks. For a moment, she looks like a young girl. "I finished my purchases and hurried home, without stopping for a treat. That night, his face came to me in a dream."

"How was it?"

She lowers her eyelids for a moment. "His complexion was pale, like the white Russians, but his hair was not blond. Actually, it was blacker than coal, and wavy. He wore no hat. His dark eyelashes shaded the most amazing eyes. They were not brown, not gray, and not green. And yet, they contained all of these colors. I've never seen anything like them since."

"Since when?"

"Since forever, Fanny. It all seems to have happened a lifetime ago. But sometimes, I feel like I could reach out to touch that time and place, and be there again."

It seems like morning will never come. Everything is so quiet. We are munching on yesterday's rolls, dangling our legs over the side of the bed. I'm waiting to hear more about the artist.

"Auntie?"

"Yes, Fanny, there is more to tell. Things at home kept me busy. My mama was pushing me to learn how to cook more dishes and to bake. She told me that before long, I would have my own kitchen to work in. There was talk about a match for me, but no date was set. The groom to be was a student from another village. I did my best, but my heart wasn't in it. At all."

"I know what you mean. The thought of a match for me made me feel helpless. I felt like a piece of challah dough, kneaded and shaped by other people."

"I tried not to think about it, as if putting it out of my mind would make it go away. You can imagine how happy I was to escape to the market on Thursdays. Each week, I skipped my treat and got closer to the art table. I looked at him only through the corner of my eye. On the fourth Thursday, I lingered at the display. I had saved enough coins to buy something. I was so intent on deciding between more paper and new pencils that I did not hear him approach. 'What would you like, Svetlana?' I looked around me, but no one else was there. It was just me and him. And then I said, 'That's not my name.' He laughed at me. He laughed at me. That made me really angry. He spoke Yiddish, but not like us. And he certainly didn't behave like any of the young men from Vahivka."

"Why did he call you Svetlana? Isn't that a Russian name?"

"I'm getting to that part, be patient. After he laughed at me, I turned to leave, but my feet didn't want to move. So I stood there, cooling off and thinking about what I would buy. Why should I let someone else's bad manners stop me from getting what I wanted? I went back to the table and began to examine the pencils. I took my time, looking at each one, picking it up, holding it up to the light, and putting it down."

"Did that make him mad?" I remember that the sellers in the marketplace didn't like you to take too long to choose.

"No, actually, he came over and began to tell me all about his life. His father had been a doctor to some important officials in Moscow, and that's why they were allowed to live there. You know, Jews were not permitted to settle in the cities or attend Russian schools. So, of course, most of us were forced to make our own way in the *shtetls*, far from their civilization."

"I know. Papa said that they only remembered us at tax time, or when they needed more young men for the army."

"True, but, because of his father's medical practice, the family had a fine home in the center of town. He went to the university, and then he was sent to Paris to study art."

"So how did he end up selling pencils in Vahivka?"

"I was wondering about that, too. He said that while he was in Paris, his father had a heart attack and died. The family was removed from their Moscow home and sent to a shtetl, far from the capital. Misha returned to Russia to help out. He started travelling around, selling art supplies and paintings when he could."

"Misha?"

"It seems that the Jews in Moscow used Russian names. He said his Jewish name was Meir."

"Misha sounds nice."

"I thought he was very nice. He showed me his paintings. They were mostly nature scenes. The things we see all around us in every season. I especially liked the pictures of trees and flowers. They were full of life. Each week, he let me sit at his easel, and he showed me how to hold a brush and apply paint to the paper."

"So it was like taking art classes."

"Not really, because I could only spend a few minutes at a time there. I had to get home with the food, and I had to be careful about gossip in the market."

"Did people look at you?"

"Not too much. As I told you, Misha's stall was at the far end of the market, just before the forest and just after Mrs. Edelman's sewing supplies. I didn't buy from her anymore. Her embroidery threads were inferior to the ones Papa brought me. Hers often broke in the middle of a stitch."

"So your papa brought you more thread, but not more paper."

"Of course. He was happy to contribute to my wedding chest. Every evening, I embroidered the edges of pillowcases and linen napkins. The trunk was filling up with all my creations. I started to work more slowly. I thought that a loaded chest would show Papa that I was ready for my wedding. I was not ready at all."

"Did you tell Misha about the match?"

"No, there was nothing to tell. I didn't have anything to do with the planning. As long as nobody said anything to me, I could continue to pretend that it wouldn't happen. Anyway, I was working on a painting of the trees next to the easel. They were pretty, but somehow they never came to life."

"What do you mean?

"I asked Misha what was missing. He said, 'Svet.' He told me that meant the light, and the reason he called me Svetlana was that he could see the light within me."

"He said that? What did you think?"

"I was amazed, and I couldn't wait for Thursday to come again."

"What happened when you returned to the market?"

"The following week, he carried the easel a few feet into the woods, and set it down. The sun's rays shone through the top leaves and spilled onto the forest floor. I was delighted with my finished painting. Without thinking, I ran over to Misha and threw my arms around him. He held my face in his two hands and lifted it up to the fading daylight. He lowered his head and let his lips touch mine for a moment. A feeling of warmth and pure happiness filled my heart."

I never dreamed my aunt could have such a secret. "Auntie, you're taking my breath away."

"I know, but then he pulled back and told me I'd be late returning to my home. He said that he would let my painting dry and give it to me the following Thursday. I didn't know how I could wait an entire week to see him again.

"As I hurried by her stand, Mrs. Edelman called out to me. She said I should wipe the paint off my cheek. I rubbed my face with the corner of my shawl and kept on walking. My mama didn't ask why I was late but told me to wash up for dinner. When my papa came home, he looked upset. On Thursday, he sent my brother to market with me. What could I do?"

"What did your brother think when he met the artist?"

"There was no artist. I could see, as soon as we arrived, that Misha's space was empty. Mrs. Edelman pointed to the vacant spot and muttered something about certain people moving around like the wind. I gave her my back and went about my business, handing the packages to my helper. I was able to buy everything we needed, in spite of the gray cloud surrounding my head and the heavy iron pressing my chest."

"Did your brother notice anything different?"

"No, he just wanted to buy a treat with the money Papa had given him. But then Shayna, the candy seller, let him take his time. While he was looking, she called me aside and gave me a yellow envelope. She told me that Misha had left it with her early that morning. My hands were trembling. I tried to slip it into my pocket, but a paper with writing fell to the floor. Mrs. Edelman walked by just in time to pick it up and hand it to me. I pushed it back into the envelope, next to my dry painting."

"Wait a minute! Is that the same envelope you put in your jacket when we left Vahivka?"

"Yes, it is."

"Really? Can I see the painting?"

"It's gone. That night, Papa came to my room, demanding to see the envelope. I gave him the picture, but I hid the letter. He threw my beautiful trees into the fireplace. He said he never had expected me to use such bad judgment. He said he thought he could trust me. He told me that my wedding was cancelled because of rumors."

"He burned your painting? That's awful. But were you at least glad the wedding was off?"

"Yes, in a way, but I was still very confused and sad. The worst thing was that I was not allowed to go to market anymore. Mama tried her best to make me happy. She taught me all her favorite cake and pastry recipes. I became a good baker, and an even better eater. I think I was drowning my sorrow in apple turnovers and almond cookies. My clothes were getting tighter. One day, I noticed Papa staring at my growing waistline and shaking his head.

"My papa was away on a selling trip for two straight weeks. When he returned, he looked very tired, and he was not alone. An older man walked in with him. Papa came right into the kitchen, leaving his companion in the sitting room. He told Mama and Shira to bring refreshments to the visitor. He said he wanted to speak to me.

"Papa explained that Avram was a respectable widower, and that he was a jeweler. I nodded my head, wondering what that had to do with me. I thought maybe Papa was sorry he burned my painting, and he wanted to buy a pair of earrings for me."

"Are those your topaz earrings?"

"No, they came later. Instead of earrings, there would be a wedding ring for me. I tried to protest, but Papa said not to worry. Avram was a kind man. He earned a good living and would be able to support me and whatever children came along."

"What did you think? Were you scared?"

"There was no time for that. The marriage ceremony took place a few days later. Avram bought a house in Vahivka, so I could be near my family. The years went by, and we made a life together."

"What do you mean by that?"

"I mean that Avram became my husband. I left my home, and the life I knew, to live with him. He was very considerate. He tried to please me. He added a room to the house for my artwork. He bought watercolors and an easel for me, but I had lost my desire for that."

"You mean you never painted again?"

"No. When Papa threw my picture into the fireplace, some of my dreams went with it."

"Do you think you'll paint in America?"

"First we have to get there. Everything has its time, Fanny."

"What happened to your painting space?"

"That became my sewing room. You know, where I embroidered and made dresses for special people." Aunt Freda points to me and smiles.

"So you see, I was content. Avram had his jewelry business as part of our house, and he let me help out. I never learned to read, but I could add numbers, and I enjoyed it when people came around. Your uncle was a good man, and he took care of me until..."

"Until when?"

"Until it was my turn to care for him. He got older and weaker. He started to forget things. One day, Alexius found him wandering in the fields. Avram was trying to find his way home from the synagogue. From then on, I arranged for Alexius to watch out for him. That was our secret. I did not want to embarrass him. In any case, I was so much younger than my husband, and I still wished I could see new places. But, I knew it was my responsibility to care for Avram. I did whatever I could to help him. He deserved that, may he rest in peace."

"Whatever happened to the student—you know, the first match they planned for you?"

"I never met him. I heard they arranged another marriage for him with a sensible girl who did not talk to strangers in the marketplace." My aunt laughs a little. A sad laugh.

"And what about Misha, Auntie?"

"Like the wind, Fanny, here and gone before you know it. I never heard about him again."

"What did the letter say?"

"Who knows? I couldn't show it to anyone, but I saved it."

"Can I see it?"

"Not now. Maybe in New York."

"Just for a minute, please, Auntie."

It's in the yellow envelope. The paper has been folded in three parts. The creases are wearing thin. I open it carefully. The letters are familiar. They are not the Yiddish or Hebrew symbols I'd seen in Louie's schoolwork or Papa's prayer books. They are not the same as the print in the Countess's magazines. They look like the signs at the train station in Kiev.

"Did Misha write in Russian?"

"Probably, since most of his studies were in Moscow."

I stare at the words, willing them to reveal their meanings. I wonder what they say. "I don't know how you could go all this time without knowing. How many years has it been?"

"Long enough, Fanny. Now give it back to me."

"Maybe someone on this ship can read it to us."

"People here have more on their minds than digging up the past. I think it's better to just forget the whole thing." *Is she kidding? What's she afraid of?*

"Can I keep it?"

"No, hand it over. We'll know what it says, someday. Maybe." My aunt tucks the envelope into her green sack and stretches her arms and legs. "Listen, Fanny."

I don't hear a sound. Oh, my goodness, the storm is over. A pale ray of sunlight is creeping under our door. It's been a long, long night. We do our best to tidy up the cabin and dress ourselves. We're both feeling a little dizzy. And hungry. I wonder if there is any breakfast to be had.

What a mess! The halls are littered with all kinds of materials, scraps of paper, pieces of metal, and wooden chips. But, mostly there is glass—chunks, shards, splinters, and even whole crystals—all over the floor. I'm trying to find clear spots to place my feet. These boots are the only ones I own. They need to last for a good while. I certainly don't want my first steps in America to be shoeless ones.

The ship's workers are scurrying around, sweeping, mopping, and picking up the remnants of last night's fierce storm. We duck around the corner and into an open doorway to avoid being mowed down by a broom almost as wide as the corridor. We find ourselves in a room we've never seen before.

This is a huge space. It's big enough to hold a wedding and invite the entire village of Vahivka. The stage, at the far end, could hold five *klezmer* bands. There is a piano, with a tail as long as a railroad wagon. But it's broken in half. A giant chandelier is lopsided and hanging from one cord. A cleaning crew enters, and they shoo us out another exit.

Now we're lost for sure. The signs, which I can't read anyway, have been tossed around. Their previously helpful arrows are now pointing aimlessly in any and all directions. I have no idea where the dining room is, but I do smell food.

I'm just not certain what kind it is. And I hear music. We follow our noses and our ears all the way out to the deck.

People are arriving from different sides of the ship, and from down below. Many have brought food with them; herring, pickles, salami, cheeses, and crackers. They are carrying breads in all shapes and sizes, and breaking off pieces to share with other passengers. Herta arrives with her helper. They are carrying massive trays of sandwiches and passing them around. The girl's braids have come undone. I notice that her pale complexion has a greenish tinge. She is struggling with her load. I walk over and take the tray out of her shaky arms.

Aunt Freda leads her over to a pile of blankets, and they sit down, side by side. When I'm finished helping Herta, I join them. We eat the cheese sandwiches as well as some fish and olives that have been offered. People are washing down their unusual breakfasts with whatever liquids are available: cold tea, lemonade, wine, and beer.

Several men are playing harmonicas. They are joined by others with fiddles, accordions, and flutes. They take turns, contributing a variety of melodies and playing together when they can. Two girls, about my age, begin a lively dance, and little by little, other passengers fall in step. My aunt is clapping her hands to the beat. It's the strangest party ever.

"What are we celebrating, Auntie?"

"Life, Fanny. It just goes on."

One day, when the deck is crowded again, we come up early to get a good view of the lady with the torch. It hardly seems that three weeks have passed since we first stepped on board, and yet, in a way, it seems that we've been here for a lifetime.

I've noticed one girl who walks around every day with a notebook and pencil, writing all the time. I never get up the courage to ask her what she was doing. I envy her ability to record our voyage, all of it. I would have so much to tell, the good times and the bad. We've had a few more storms, but nothing like our second day at sea. Many people get sick. Some get better, and some do not. Two babies are born during our trip. One boy and one girl. I never get to see them, but I hear that both have been named "America."

Most days, my aunt and I join many others on deck. It is a great reprieve, especially for the passengers cramped down below in steerage. Among those are Malka and her family. We have become friends. I help out with her younger sisters and brother. She tells me they are headed for Philadelphia. I will miss her. It would have been nice if they were settling in New York, so I could begin my new life here with one friend.

Aunt Freda spends most of her time sewing. I have grown a little, and she lets out a few of my blouses. Her clothes have to be taken in a bit. She is happy about that and uses the trimmings to make dolls for some of the little girls. She dresses them in tiny copies of the fashions in her magazines.

The three sisters hover around my aunt, admiring her skills. One of them hands her a small card. It has printed letters on it, and some numbers, too. She points to it and says something very slowly and clearly. I think it might be English. "I am recommended." Then she repeats it. "I am recommended."

My aunt thanks her and slips the card into her sack. Later, in our cabin, we examine the sister's card. My aunt admires the textured white paper and the lovely letters. They are printed in a shiny shade of blue. They are slightly raised and feel bumpy under my fingertips.

"Very fancy card, Fanny, but why did she give it to me? I wonder what it says. Oh well." Aunt Freda pushes the card under her clothes, and tries to imitate the phrase that the sister repeated so seriously. We say it over and over, shaking our heads, until we collapse with laughter.

Last night we had another party. There was not too much food left, but there was plenty of music and dancing. We sat with a group of women we had met in the dining room. My aunt looked happy and relaxed. Her feet tapped to the beat. A tall man came over and extended his hand. She told him she couldn't dance, because the mourning period for her husband was not yet finished.

I guess he didn't understand what she said, because he led her over to a circle of dancers. They pulled her around with them as they moved faster and faster to the varying rhythms. When she finally returned to her seat, her cheeks were pink and moist. My aunt was smiling.

We slept very little after that, and here we are, along with so many others, craning our necks. Last-minute good-byes and good lucks surround me. People are asking each other where they will be staying. From what I hear, some will be traveling more, taking trains to unheard of places like Arkansas and Ohio.

Most of us will be staying with family members and even relations of our relatives. People who have arrived before us are expected to take in newcomers, just as they were received in their time. It seems like a never-ending chain. Maybe one day, we'll be able to send for Louie and Papa, and, oh yes, Ida. For now, it's our turn to be welcomed.

Voices are calling out to the statue in many languages. I wonder which ones she understands. Some people are jumping up and down and waving their arms in the air. Others are just standing still and pointing in her direction. But she's looking straight at me, only me. Really, she is.

Her right arm is raised and holds her famous torch. I had heard about that. But her left arm is wrapped around a huge book! I stare up at her beautiful face and her kind eyes. They seem to be saying, "Fanny, I've been waiting for you. Come and read. Your turn has come."

"Thank you, Lady," I whisper.

SEVEN

A NEW WORLD

Aunt Freda calls out, "Sophie, Mendel," and points to the shore. I'm wondering how my aunt can find her relatives in this mass of people, all craning their necks, waiting for the ship to arrive. And then I see them, too.

Uncle Avram's cousin is shaped like a matzo ball, but not the kind that Mama used to make. Hers were soft and fluffy, floating on the simmering soup. Sophie resembles the sinking kind, round, but with a hard core. She's staring straight ahead. The set of her mouth is a straight line of dissatisfaction. Her husband is busy looking all around him. He has the kind of eyes that make me feel uncomfortable. I don't know why.

My aunt tries in vain to attract their attention. Her arms are lost in the midst of so many others waving to their *landsmen*. The sound of her voice is swallowed up in the horns and blasts of the small boats that surround us. These little vessels seem to be guiding our ship, and some are even pushing it into the harbor.

I hear a loud thud as we hit the dock and a deafening clang as the anchor drops. Some of the passengers are shoving each other, trying to get to the gangplank. They are pushed aside by a band of uniformed men marching onto the deck.

"Oh my gosh, Auntie, is the Czar's army here in New York, too?"

She laughs. "No, silly, these must be American guards." Still, she takes a few steps back when they approach. The first thing the officials do is to herd all the steerage passengers down below again. Malka had told me that their group would not be let off right away. They will be taken to another place for health exams first.

We are told to stand in line. I watch as the doctors examine the eyes of each newcomer while one of the officers glances at the documents. A few people are not allowed to leave. They are sent down below to wait with the steerage passengers. When one family member is held back, others cry out and often join them.

"Auntie, what's happening?"

"Shah, Fanny, be calm. Don't show that you're afraid. Just follow me. And by the way, I need to tell you something about Sophie and Mendel."

"I saw them. They're waiting for us."

"Well, not exactly. They're waiting for me and for... Avram."

"Don't they know?"

"No, I couldn't take a chance. How could I ask someone to write a letter for me? Don't worry, they owe me this. It was Avram who gave them the money to come here five years ago. It will be all right. Trust me, Fanny. Remember, when I asked you to come with me, I promised to take care of you."

The doctor pokes my eyelid with a wooden stick. It hurts. I cover it with my free hand. He yanks my hand away and stares into my eye through a glass lens. Aunt Freda has already passed inspection. I see her just ahead of me. She's standing perfectly still. She doesn't even reach for a hankie to wipe the beads of sweat forming on her upper lip and her brow. For a moment, everything stops. It's like we're frozen in time. Then, I see one of the uniformed men motion to the doctor and call out a command. It must be English. It sounds like *Urriup*. I'm allowed to join my aunt. She grabs my arm and lets out a sigh of relief.

As soon as we reach the end of the gangplank, I plant my right foot onto the ground. I'm not really superstitious, but many people back in Vahivka believed that you should always enter a new place right foot first. Anyhow, it can't hurt. I'm conscious of each step I take, right, left, right. I can't seem to steady myself. My legs are wobbly, and I feel a little dizzy. I think the three weeks of ocean waves have not left my body. I try to straighten my spine, but I'm really tired and nervous. People around us are greeting their relatives with handshakes, hugs, and some tears.

"Freda, Freda, look, here we are. Where's Avram?"

That's a big voice from such a short person. Pushing through the crowd is not easy, but at last we are standing in front of Sophie and her husband. There are no embraces for us. Not even a smile.

"So, Freda, what have you done with my cousin, and why is this girl here?"

Not very welcoming words. A knot is forming in my throat.

"Take it easy, Sophie, I'll tell you everything when we get to your home."

"What do you mean, we? The 'we' I expected was Avram and you." My aunt takes a deep breath and looks up to the sky.

"Sophie, Mendel, this is my niece, Fanny Tatch, my sister Shira's daughter." I lower my eyes but try to smile. "And..." Another deep breath from my aunt. "You knew that Avram was in poor health. He took a turn for the worse shortly before our journey. It wasn't possible to inform you of his passing."

"And the girl?" My chin begins to tremble. I position my-self behind Aunt Freda's long skirt, and I turn my head away to hide a few tears. I can see our ship pulling out of the port. For a split second, I feel like running to catch it to return to Vahivka. Then I see the lady with her torch and book. My body aches, but I use whatever strength remains to straight-en up and stand next to my aunt. She puts her arm around me and gives me a squeeze.

"Fanny is with me. Now, let's get moving. We're very tired."

"Mendel, help Freda with her bag. The girl can manage her own."

I glance back at the statue, and it seems that she's wink-ing at me!

We walk a few blocks, trying to get away from the mob of people near the dock. My satchel gets heavier with every step I take. Eventually, Mendel steps into the middle of the road and signals to one of the wagon drivers to pull over. First he heaves his wife into a seat, then he helps Aunt Freda, and finally he grabs my hand and elbow.

"Let her get in herself. She's young enough."

Mendel releases my arm and settles himself next to the driver. Each street we pass has rows of buildings on both sides. Some are low, one or two levels, and others are quite tall. I try to count the floors as we go by. I get as high as six stories!

My eyelids are beginning to droop. My head falls into the back of the bench. The New York streets fade from view. The horse's clip-clop rhythm rocks me to sleep. I'm dreaming that I'm on the bumpy road to Kiev. Alexius is coaxing Luba to pull the cart just a little while longer. His gentle voice sud-denly changes into Sophie's shrill one. "So she's sleeping al-ready. Let her rest. Tomorrow we'll be up bright and early. I have a job set up for you, Freda. You'll be one of the seam-stresses. I hope you don't disappoint."

"What are you talking about? You know I can sew." I can hear the frustration in my aunt's tone. I decide to keep my eyes shut.

"This is not your fancy stitchery, my dear. This is hard work. When we arrived, years ago, I was glad to get such a job. I almost broke my back, bending over that heavy machine. Now, I'm the forelady. No more sitting for me. I walk the floor making sure the girls are pulling their weight."

"Sewing...machines?"

"Get used to the modern world, Freda. You had a comfortable life with Avram. But that was then. By the way, did he leave any jewelry for me? There must have been a lot left from his shop."

"Too dangerous for the journey." Aunt Freda does not mention the earrings and rings sewn into some of her garments.

"Mmm, so you arrive here with nothing but another mouth to feed. She'll have to work, too. You can start paying me for your room and meals next Friday."

"Slow down, Sophie. Remember, it was my husband who paid your way to America."

"That was his gift to me. It has nothing to do with you."

"All right. I'm not afraid of hard work, but Fanny will be going to school."

"Not while she's under my roof. Let her do her share. She's not the daughter of a countess."

Mendel bursts out laughing. Then he stops himself. "Enough already, Sophie, you're annoying the horse."

⌒‿⌐

We eat a cold, silent meal in Sophie's cramped kitchen. The borsht is pale-pink and watery. I almost gag on the bitter beets. I'm glad we're only allotted a tiny portion of herring. The bread is almost as hard as the bed we're to sleep in.

"Be glad you have your own room. Most newcomers are happy to get a cot in the kitchen." Sophie tosses a second flat cushion on our bed. I long for the fluffy, feather-stuffed pillow I left behind.

My first morning in America finds me achy and still grimy from the journey. I carry a change of clothes, a sliver of soap, and a thin towel down the dark hallway to the communal washroom. The odor overpowers me. I don't know whether to clean the bathroom or myself first. Almost as soon as I enter, someone starts banging on the door and calling out in a language I don't recognize.

I finish washing and dressing as quickly as I can. By the time I release the chain lock, a line has formed outside the door. Some of the people look worn out, even though the day is just beginning. Mostly, they are looking down, or sideways at the grungy wallpaper. One older woman directs her gaze to me.

"So, *sheyne meydl,* you new here?"

It's been a long time since anyone has called me a pretty girl. I feel my cheeks turning red. "We arrived yesterday."

"Ah, so much to learn here. Some lessons are not that easy. You'll be all right. What's your name?"

"Fanny."

"I'm Sarah. Good luck..." I start to head back down the hall, when I hear Sarah's voice again. "Fanny, a piece of advice for you. Everyone is going to tell you what to do, even those who just got off the boat a week before you did. They all think that they have the right answers. You can't listen to them all. The decisions will have to be your own. Learn to trust yourself." Before I can say thanks, she takes her turn to use the washroom.

The unsmiling Sophie removes some bread from a bag. Each slice is an exact square. She smears some purple gelatin over the top and places two pieces on my plate. She thumps down a thick mug, spilling some of the brown, milky liquid. I'm trying to force it all down.

"Stop staring at your food and start eating. We don't have all day." When Sophie turns away, I lean over to Aunt Freda.

"What is this?"

Sophie is the one to respond. "*This*, my dear girl, is an American breakfast, quick and tasty. We don't have time here to be kneading our own bread and picking berries for jam. I, for one, am happy to be modern."

I'm thinking that Sophie was never a good cook. The perfectly shaped bread has reduced itself to a pasty glob at the back of my mouth and refuses to be washed down with the lukewarm coffee. I lift a paper napkin to my lips and cough the remains into it. I use a second tissue to wipe my chin.

"Take it easy, those things cost money. Here, we work hard and learn to count every penny." A piece of the crust is still caught in my throat. I gulp down the last drop in my cup and get ready to leave. Whatever awaits us cannot possibly be worse than our morning meal.

Sophie has been talking nonstop since we left her small apartment. The staircase and hallway are so dark that the sudden sunlight blinds me for a moment. It's early morning, but the street is bustling with life. Mama would have called it a *lebedik velt*. That's what she sometimes said on a busy market day. She should see this world! "Is market day always on Monday, Tante Sophie?"

"I'm not your aunt, little girl, and this is how Hester Street looks every day of the week—and Orchard Street, too. You certainly have a lot to learn."

"So I've been told," I mumble. I don't know how to address her. In Vahivka, we always referred to older relatives and family friends as aunt and uncle. Maybe I'll try to avoid speaking to her altogether.

I'm busy looking around me and trying not to bump into any of the carts or people. Brick buildings lean against wooden ones. They vary in height from three to six stories. Most of the windows are open. I can see women leaning on some of the windowsills, and clothes draped over others. What they all have in common are small shops on street level. Each little store has an overhang of cloth in front. A variety of items hang from these awnings.

As if that were not enough, the middle of the road is lined with stalls and pushcarts, offering merchandise of every sort. I see young boys balancing large bundles of clothing over their skinny shoulders. Women wrapped in shawls are picking at produce, bargaining with the vendors, and reaching into worn change purses for a few pennies. They place their meager purchases in baskets slung over their arms. The men are almost all wearing stylish hats, with rounded tops and curled up brims. They rush by us.

"They're the lucky ones," Sophie tells my aunt. "They have jobs. It doesn't matter how much education they have, or what they did in the old country. Here, mostly, they work in garment shops, like mine."

She acts like she owns the business. I wonder what kind of job Mendel has. Happily, he was gone before we woke up.

I don't have to wonder for long. Sophie is bragging about the skilled job that keeps her husband employed. Something to do with cutting glass at an uptown factory. That's why he leaves early in the morning. Good.

Every once in a while, a horse-drawn cart manages to find a path from one end of the street to the other. Every corner has a tall metal pole with a sign on it. I have no idea what the letters say, but I remember that Sophie's building is on Hester Street. We walk a few blocks, turn a corner, and stop in front of a building like any other. "Here we are." She points to a placard in the first floor window. "Ludlow Industries," she enunciates. I notice that the first word is the same as the name on the corner pole. This must be Ludlow Street.

I can hear the hum before we even open the door. It gets louder as we enter. Inside are two long tables of women sitting across from each other, bent over the buzzing machines. I count twenty-four workers on this floor. A few are not much older than I am, and others appear to be Aunt Freda's age. Some are blondes, others are brunettes, but all of them wear their hair pulled up and held in place with combs and ribbons. The women are wearing blouses and long skirts covered with aprons. I can see beads of perspiration rolling down their necks and moistening their shirts.

I notice that the floor is littered with fabric scraps, pieces of thread, and pins. It is quite warm in here. I see that all the windows are bolted down. I would like to ask why, but I don't want to engage her in conversation. The workers barely look up when we arrive, but they seem to stiffen as Sophie approaches the tables. "Gut morenink, leadees." I guess she speaks English. I'm impressed. They nod their heads but keep at their tasks.

We follow Sophie up a rickety staircase. There is a smaller workroom here. A few ladies are seated at a table, sewing by hand. There are no machines at all. I notice a man, about Papa's age, at the far end of the floor. He is writing in a giant notebook. As I get closer to his desk, I can see that he's recording columns of numbers. He has yellow paper folded and clipped over the cuffs of his white shirt. That's nice. Less scrubbing for his wife on laundry day. "So where is Mr. Blum? I told him I was bringing my relative to work here."

"I'm to handle this, Sophie." The gentleman rises and bows to us. "Welcome to our shop, ladies." He speaks a cultured form of Yiddish. An educated man.

My aunt smiles. "Please, call me Freda. This is my niece, Fanny."

"Let me do the talking, Freda, I'm the one getting you this job."

"I think they need you on the floor, Sophie." He does not raise his voice, but he is firm. "I have instructions from Mr. Blum, himself. Leave the ladies to me."

"When is the boss returning? I'd like to have a word with him."

"Suit yourself, Sophie."

As soon as she is gone, the man pulls out two chairs for us to sit.

My aunt clears her throat. I can tell she's nervous. "Sir," she begins.

"Please, call me Mike."

"Mike?" She can't help staring at him.

"Well, actually, it's Meyer, but Mike is more American." He laughs a bit.

"Meyer?' Aunt Freda shakes her head and straightens her back. Where have I heard that name before? Oh, yes, Misha. Mama was right, life is a circle.

Mike keeps us with him for quite a while, asking questions about our experience. Mama always said the truth is best. My aunt confesses that she's never worked at a machine in her life, but she can sew anything by hand. I tell him that I don't like to sew, and I really want to go to school. "What to do?" he asks himself. He has very kind eyes. I can't read a book, but I've learned to read faces.

After a while, he stands up. "You'll start tomorrow, Freda. You will sit upstairs with the finishers, hand stitching the last details on the garments." He glances at the numbers in his book. "I can start you at six cents an hour, and see how it goes."

My aunt nods her head and thanks him.

"You, Fanny, can attend school in the morning and report here after class, to sweep up all the trimmings. We can pay you ten cents for three hours each day. Tell Sophie to help you register at the public school."

I lower my head. "She says no school for me, only work."

Mike raises his eyebrows and calls out, "David!" A smiling young man appears out of nowhere. He tips his cap, revealing a tumble of amber-colored curls. Every time Mike says something to him, David repeats the same word. It sounds like *fain*.

After a while, Mike turns to us and switches to Yiddish. "David is a helper here. He runs errands for us. He's been here for several years. He's a good boy, and you can trust him. He only speaks English. He's from Ireland. I can't leave the factory, so he'll show you around and help Fanny start school." What can we do? We're in his care for a while. Mike reaches into his pocket and hands David a few coins. "Lonch," he says and sends us off.

As we get closer to the door, it sounds like the machines are screaming in pain. Sophie is marching back and forth on her short round legs, peering over the workers' shoulders. David does not stop to greet her but keeps walking. We're not quick enough.

Her piercing voice rises above the racket. "Where are you going, and why is he with you? Didn't Meyer give you work? I'm going to speak to the boss about this. Who does he think he is? Doesn't he realize how important I am to the running of this factory?" Sophie does not wait for an answer. She just keeps on with her rant. "I'll take care of this, don't you worry. In the meantime, come here, so I can show you how to operate the machine." We walk over, reluctantly, to update Sophie on our new jobs. I hope my aunt doesn't mention anything about the school for now.

"Sophie, Mike did give us jobs. We start—"

"You can begin now. Watch Carmela carefully. She's one of the best here." Sophie nudges the young woman seated in front of us. She is hunched over the arm of a shiny black metal machine. It is shaped like the bent limb of a tree. It has beautifully curved gold letters painted from one end to other. Carmela is a pretty name. I've never heard it before. She is pulling cloth over a flat surface a few inches below the arm, finishing seams in record time. I look around. Everyone is doing the same thing, and forming piles of partially sewn garments in the center of the table. But the chosen Carmela is really the fastest.

"Gedup," Sophie orders the young woman. Carmela wipes her brow with the skirt of her apron, and rises. "Freda, *zetsn zikh*." Sophie points to the vacated chair. My aunt does not move. "I'm too old to be told where to sit. We're leaving for now. I'll see you later at home."

Some of the women start to giggle. They are the ones who understand our language. Sophie's mouth opens, but no words escape.

"Sophie, go help Angela with the threads." It's Mike. I never heard him coming. Who could hear footsteps over this constant racket? Angela's machine is the last one at the second long table. An empty spool is rotating rapidly on a stubby metal rod, perched at the top of the arm. Sophie wobbles over, waving her arms and yelling at the poor girl. She's able to stop the machine, remove the spool, and attach a fresh one without once looking away from us. I watch in amazement as she weaves the new thread in and out of the metal attachments, leading to a bobbing needle at the end. My aunt is shaking at the sight. Tears are running down Angela's hollow cheeks. Mike walks over and hands her his handkerchief.

Then he turns his attention to Aunt Freda, who is losing all of her color. "Angela is new here. She'll learn. Some take longer than others to catch on." Angela, another pretty name.

Sophie places both hands on her hips. "Some never learn. I hope you do better, Freda." My aunt is shaking her head vigorously and backing away from the tables.

"Where are you going?" demands Sophie.

Mike shoos us toward the door. "Take it easy, Sophie. They both have jobs, beginning tomorrow."

"Why are they going out with David? He doesn't even speak Yiddish!"

"They'll be fine. He'll show them around the neighborhood a bit and take them to your building later on."

"Show them around? They're not on holiday, and this isn't Paris!" Those are the last words I hear before we reach the street. I wonder if Mike is going to tell her about the school. I guess we'll find out tonight.

My aunt walks between us. It's only proper. Even though no one knows us here, we don't want to start off badly. So she's the chaperone, but not the leader. That was David. "Dovid," a good Jewish name, but Mike says he's from a country called Ireland. He speaks English. Good for him. Good for me, too, I hope.

The streets are busier than before, even though there are fewer children around. Maybe they're in school. Ah, school. At one time, the chance of me ever going to a class to learn to read was as likely as being able to fly. And yet I feel the fluttering of wings somewhere deep inside me. I look up to the bright sky.

My aunt grabs my arm. "Watch your step, Fanny." I look down. The cobblestone streets are scattered with puddles of murky water, droppings from the passing horses, and vegetable trimmings and discarded fish heads tossed out of the vendors' pushcarts. The odors mix and rise up to my nostrils. I cover my nose with the edge of my cape. David bursts out laughing and says a few words. I wish I knew what they were. I do understand some of the sellers, because they offer their wares in Yiddish.

"Fresh carp, white fish! You'll make the best gefilte fish in New York!"

"Cabbage, two cents a head, you won't find it for less!"

"*Shabbos* candles, two for a penny! Five cents for a dozen. Get them today. Make sure you're ready for the Sabbath!"

"Come, ladies," an older man calls out, "buy stockings, top quality, very cheap. Have a look."

My aunt glances at his stand and shrugs. "Next week," she tells him, "when I get my first pay."

"Ah, a newcomer, and you've got a job already. *Mazel tov.*"

She straightens her shoulders. "I start tomorrow."

Some boys are not in school, I see. They are salesmen of a sort, peddling a variety of newspapers that they drag around in wide cotton sacks. I hear their young voices over the din, calling out the latest headlines, some in Yiddish, others in English, I guess, and maybe other languages, too. I don't stop to listen. I want to get to the school as soon as possible. It's true we only arrived yesterday, but I've been waiting a lifetime for this chance.

We are still on Ludlow Street. I recognize the same sign on each corner. Somehow, we manage to traverse three long blocks without soiling our boots or skirts. At the fourth corner, we turn right. David notices that I'm staring at the street sign. This one has so many letters. "Rivington," he says. Then he says it again, slowly this time, "Riv-eeng-ton Stree-eet." I try to repeat it just the way he said it. This makes him laugh again. It's fun to be in the company of such a cheerful person.

We stop in the middle of this block, right in front of a wide brick building. It takes up the rest of the street. I see a flag flying above the tall windows on the fourth floor. It's made of silk, with red and white stripes. A patch of blue sky, studded with white stars, rests in the upper left-hand corner. So pretty. I feel as if it's waving me in.

There is a steep stone stairway in the center of the school, leading up to a pair of tall bronze doors. Large letters are etched across the top. David reads aloud. "Pub-lick Skoo-ool too-wen-tee."

My heart is beating wildly. I take a deep breath and try to repeat the name of this sacred place. "Poo-lit shul tootee." I shake my head. I know it's not right.

David smiles. "Cum long, Fanny, it'll be fain." I like the way he says my name.

Getting in:
This is a large room, with many windows. It should be airy, but actually, it's stuffy in here. Only one of the windows is open—at the top, and just a crack.

There are three wooden desks. The biggest is front and center, just behind a long counter. There are two in the rear, to the left and right of the main desk.

The first woman I see sits importantly in her tall chair. Her silver hair is pulled back into a tight bun held in place by white hairpins. She peers over the top of her spectacles. "Sit-t," she commands, pointing to the straight-backed bench behind us. We wait, hands folded, ankles crossed, except for David, who keeps both feet flat on the floor.

I know it's not polite to stare, but I'm really curious. I keep my eyelids slightly lowered, but I look at the other women. The one seated on the left is bent over a clicking machine. Her fingers pat the round tabs. Every once in a while, a little bell rings, and her left hand presses on a lever, which pushes a paper-covered cylinder to the right. The paper rises with every push, and then she pulls it off the tube. David leans across my aunt. "Tai-ping," he whispers. *Tai-ping,* I repeat in my head.

The lady to the right rises and walks to a narrow metal chest. She opens the top drawer and removes a stiff sheet of paper. She brings it over to the counter, wrapping her sweater tightly around her thin torso. She glances at the open window and frowns. Her frown does not change to a smile, as she beckons to us. "Nay-m," she says, without looking at us.

"Fanny Tatch," says David. Now the woman raises her head and points to me with her yellow pencil.

"Nay-m," she repeats in a loud squeaky voice. My aunt pokes me. "*Der nomen*," she says.

I know. I clear my throat. "Fanny Tatch." It doesn't even sound like my own voice. It's quiet, even for me. "Speek op!" This time the woman yells, as if that will help.

I think I'm going to faint. A cold sweat begins at my hairline and works its way down to my neck. My body begins to tremble slightly, and my knees feel wobbly. I have an urge to run out of this impressive building, but where would I go? I hear the impatient tapping of the official pencil, ready to begin its work. The rhythm puts words in my head. *It's your turn, it's your turn, it's your turn.*

"Fanny Tatch," I holler. The tai-ping lady laughs out loud, while the skinny one writes on the large card, which she places on her desk. Then, she marks some numbers on a slip of paper and hands it to me.

"T'morro morning, ayt ay em." She turns her back to us.

David must see the worry lines forming on my forehead. He takes the paper from me, turns it over, and draws a clock. He makes the hands show eight o'clock. "Ta-ma-ro moorning," he says, pointing to his illustration. Ah, *morgn*. I get it. I have to return to the school at eight o'clock with the paper. I'm in!

On our way out of the building, I see lines of children marching down the hall. Boys and girls together. Each pair of lines seems to consist of children of the same age. Every once in a while, I see an older student walking at the end of a younger class. The smaller boys are dressed in knee-length pants and white shirts. The girls are wearing skirts that fall below their knees, but not as far down as their ankles. All of a sudden, my skirt feels way too long. Most of the little girls have their hair parted down the middle, with two braids in the back. The older girls also have center parts, but not braids. Their hair is pulled back and tied with ribbons. Just like in the photo of the American classroom.

I remember my rainbow of ribbons, left behind in Vahivka. They were Manya's gift to me for my thirteenth birthday, almost two years ago. That was before Manya moved away, before Mama passed away, and Uncle Avram, too. Before Ida arrived, and before I left for good. But, here we are, and tomorrow will be my turn to learn.

The sun is high in the sky. This was the time I prepared Papa's lunch each day and brought it to him in his shop. I wonder who is doing that for him now, and I wonder when we will eat. My stomach is beginning to rumble, really. I think David hears it, because he laughs, again. "Soon, Fanny," he says.

I don't know what he means, but somehow, I am reassured.

Aunt Freda and I follow him, retracing our steps. I hope we're not going back to the sewing factory again. Mike had said we start tomorrow. I see some of the same vendors still at their pushcarts. The stocking man is sitting next to his, but his eyes are buried in a book. As we get closer, I can see it is a prayer book like Papa and Louie had. He is a learned man. Selling stockings. I'm a little surprised when my aunt walks over to him. We don't have any cash, and I heard her tell him she'd be back next week. Maybe she's going to ask him to save a pair for her till then. David and I are right behind her. The old man looks up reluctantly as Aunt Freda begins to speak. "Reb, do you have some hair ribbons?" He rifles through his meager merchandise, and holds up three colored ones. My aunt examines them. "Which one do you want, Fanny?"

I stare at them. "Yellow," I whisper.

"Speak up; you're a schoolgirl now."

"Ah, a schoolgirl, good for you."

The man folds the yellow ribbon in four, slips it into a small paper bag, and hands it to me. "Thank you, Reb, I'll be back next week to pay you, and to buy my stockings." He nods his head, reaches into his cart, and offers me a honey-colored candy. "This is for your first day at school, so you'll always remember that learning is sweet."

David leads the way, pointing to street signs as we go. He seems to know how to weave his way in and out of the crowds. The tea shop is almost as bustling as the street out-side. "Al-len Street," David informs me. We find a small square table in the far corner. The aromas here remind me of home—I mean, the home I left. I hear snippets of Yiddish words in slightly different accents.

It's nice that David was thoughtful enough to choose a place like this, or maybe Mike had suggested it. When the server appears, David indicates to my aunt that she should order. He hands her the money that Mike had given him. She stares at the coins. We have no idea of their value. Aunt Freda shows them to the waiter and confers with him brief-ly. After a while, we are presented with a platter of blintzes and knishes and three glasses of tea.

"Mmm." David likes the knish. He gobbles one down, and starts on a second.

"Knish," I inform him. "Po-tay-toe," he replies.

I repeat it. I'm learning English. David may work as an er-rand boy for the factory, but he is a good teacher. I'm eating a lot, too. Better to fill up now. Who knows what kind of "quick and tasty" supper Sophie will offer us.

Our shadows greet us as we exit the restaurant. The peo-ple filling the streets now are dragging their feet. Some are purchasing the afternoon papers from boys calling out the latest news. I can only understand the Yiddish headlines. Something about Jewish people leaving Russia because of in-creasing attacks on their villages. *Oh, please, not in Vahivka,* I pray. There were pogroms in neighboring shtetls before I left. I wish Papa and Louie were with us in New York. Maybe one day. "Everything in time," Mama used to say.

I'm beginning to recognize a few street signs. The block after Allen is called Orchard. David stops in front of a small store. "Wait." He puts up one hand. I think I know what he means. *Way-t*, I say to myself. David enters the shop and returns shortly with a thin package and a broad smile.

We follow again, without knowing where we are going. This is frustrating and fun, all at the same time. The block after Orchard is Ludlow, where Sophie works, but we don't stop. The street after that is called Essex. I look at the sign, while David pronounces it, "Ess-ex."

Hidden among the narrow, cramped streets of Manhattan lives and breathes a delightful park. Mothers are rocking their babies to sleep under lovely trees. I take a deep breath. Nice. Toddlers are playing in the grass. We find an unoccupied bench, and we sit, my aunt in the middle, as always. She leans back and closes her eyes. David unties the thin cord of his package and folds back the brown wrapper to reveal a new copybook.

Its cover has a black-and-white marble design with a blank space right in the center. A yellow pencil rolls out and falls to the ground. I watch as David retrieves it and dusts it off. He takes a small metal object from his pocket and pulls out a tiny knife from its side. He uses the point to sharpen the lead pencil. Then, very carefully, he writes on the front of the notebook, pronouncing each letter aloud. "ef-ay-en-en-ooai-tee-ay-tee-see-aych." The letters are written neatly, straight across the white area of the book. David points to me. "FANNY TATCII," my own name, in print. I swallow.

David turns to the last page in the copybook. He draws lines from top to bottom and from left to right. Then he pencils in street signs where the lines meet and writes on each one. I recognize most of the names as he says them aloud. Next, he makes a few sketches on several of the penciled streets and labels them. He writes three large letters at the top of the page and holds the book up to admire his work.

"Fur you, Fanny." David reaches across my aunt and hands me the book and then the pencil. "A gift," he says and bows a little. Aunt Freda opens her eyes, and then her mouth, when she sees what I have. "*A dank*," I tell David, quietly. He knows what I mean. "Thaink-eiu," he says. That's an important word to learn. I repeat it. I am feeling thankful, and hopeful, and happy.

David stands and leads us out of the park. As we walk along, my eyes dart back and forth between the actual street signs and the drawing in my new copybook. When we turn onto Hester Street, I know where we are headed, and I close the notebook, mentally tucking my hopes and dreams inside. Until tomorrow.

"Fanny, what do you have in your hand?" I look up. It's Sarah, the lady I met this morning on my way to the washroom. She's sitting on the right side of the steps with two other women. People are passing on the left, entering the shabby building with bundles of their own. I can see through their mesh bags just what they have, a newspaper, a loaf of bread, a jar of pickles, a hunk of cheese.

But my package is the most precious. To me. "Look, it's my copybook. And I have a pencil." I forget my shy ways.

"Very nice, Fanny. So you know how to write?"

"Not really, not yet, but...*tomorrow* I'll start to learn. It will be my first day of school."

"You mean your first day of *work*, dear girl."

Sophie pushes past the women and grabs my notebook. I yank it out of her hand and hold it to my chest.

"*Redn nisht*, Fanny, I'll take care of this."

"Don't worry," I tell my aunt, "I'm not talking to her at all." I begin to cough. My chest is tightening around my pounding heart. The knot in my throat is growing harder. I take a deep, deep breath, close my eyes, and try to picture the lovely green park on Essex Street, where David wrote my name.

And I let Aunt Freda speak for me. "Good evening, Sophie, how was your day?"

"Never mind *my* day. How was your little holiday? Nice, I hope, because tomorrow starts your real life here. You have to work, make money, and pay your rent. Forget about school. I heard that people in your family always thought they were special, and I can see that hasn't changed."

"In our family, we don't air our dirty laundry in public."

"Of course you don't. You've kept it hidden for a long time."

"I don't know what you're talking about."

"I think you do."

My aunt is turning red. I don't know if she's angry or embarrassed. I don't even know what Sophie means, or why she's talking like this. The women are staring at us.

Sarah frowns at the accuser and pulls me aside. She whispers in my ear, "Don't worry your head, Fanny. Save your head for your lessons. I never told a soul, but going to school was always a dream for me. An impossible dream for a girl in my shtetl. It can happen for you here. Don't let her kind stop you." She points at Sophie. "Do it for yourself and for all of us who never had a chance." Sarah smiles at me. One lone tear rolls down a crease in her cheek.

Monday evening:

Mendel is seated at the kitchen table, with a newspaper spread out in front of him. It looks like the same journal that the boy was selling on Orchard Street. The Yiddish one. I want to ask him about the pogroms, but I don't really want to speak directly to him, and especially not to Sophie. So I keep still. But not my aunt. "Good evening, Mendel." Aunt Freda always remembers her manners. It seems that Mendel forgot his, or maybe he never had any. He hardly looks up from his reading, just nods his head. My aunt walks over to our room and lies down on the bed.

Sophie busies herself around the small kitchen and puts another cold meal on the table. A plate of sardines, sitting in a pool of oil, a cut-up onion, and a loaf of rye bread, cut into thick slices. I'm glad I had a hearty lunch.

Sophie sets down four plates and an assortment of utensils. She pauses for a moment and calls out, "Freda, come. Sit down and eat. Forget about what I said before. The past is the past. I, for one, would never fault you for the scandal."

What is she talking about? My aunt takes her seat, head slightly lowered. Still, I can see a few tears ready to fall. Maybe it's the onions. Maybe it's Sophie. "Mendel, stop reading. It's time to eat." He snaps the paper right in front of me and closes it. He startles me. I gasp.

"Oh, a delicate creature, I see." He makes a pouting movement with his lips.

Sophie laughs at his joke. "She was not too delicate to spend an entire day parading around the city with that young Irisher from the factory."

Mendel winks at me. I feel like crawling away. Instead, I stare at the supper and decide on a piece of bread. Sophie can't let well enough alone. "Better give her some advice, Freda. You don't want her following in your footsteps, do you?"

"Enough, Sophie, let her be." Mendel picks up his newspaper. Tears are streaming down my aunt's reddening cheeks. I forget my shyness, and my vow of silence, and speak up. "Stop bothering Aunt Freda. Why are you treating her this way? Everyone in the village loves and respects her."

"Not our family. We have our reasons."

"Your cousin Bertha says that my aunt took wonderful care of Uncle Avram."

"Really?" Sophie shakes her head in disbelief.

Mendel lowers his paper and clears his throat. "Of course she would say that. The house and everything in it was left to her."

My aunt looks up suddenly and wipes her tearstained face. She stands and points at Mendel.

Sophie rises, too, and stands directly in front of her husband. "How on earth would you know such a thing?"

Mendel remains seated. He's wringing his hands. "I heard it from someone."

"And who would that someone be? There are no landsmen here in this building. No one who knew Bertha or anyone else in my family."

"Maybe I heard it at work."

"From whom?"

"A new worker. I forget his name."

"Liar!" She's screaming, now. "Tell me now how you know this, and for how long."

I'm sure that Sarah and the other neighbors can hear her. I feel ashamed.

Mendel tries to get up, but Sophie pushes him back down with both hands. She lowers her voice and speaks to him in a slow, steady way, as if to a child. "Mendel Resnick, you know you can't keep a secret for long. Just tell me what you've been hiding, and for what reason." Sophie's quiet voice is even scarier than the loud version. Mendel must know that. Sweat is dripping down from the top of his balding head to his collar. He wipes his neck with a napkin and pushes his chair away from the table. He pulls a blackened metal key from his pants pocket and walks over to a desk in the hall. His hand is shaking so badly, he can't seem to fit the key in the lock.

Sophie wobbles over and grasps the key with her chubby fingers. She has no trouble opening the desktop. She picks up an envelope from the top of a pile of papers inside and holds it out. "And what can this be?" Her shrill voice is back.

"It's a letter, Sophie, addressed to me. It arrived just a few days ago, and I put it away for safekeeping. I guess I forgot about it until now."

"Is that so?" Sophie's grip tightens. She studies the envelope for a few minutes and finally hands it over. For just a moment, I feel sorry for Sophie. She's losing her power. She can't read it, of course. She has to depend on Mendel for that. I can't read either, but I do recognize the stationery. And the red wax stamp on the tip of the flap!

"It's from my papa!"

"Yes it is, little girl, but it's for me. See, here's my name, right on the front of the envelope." Mendel grins at me. He places the envelope on the table and extracts several sheets of paper. Sophie pokes his outstretched hand with her elbow. The paper quivers.

"Read it, Mendel, and start from the beginning. I want to hear everything."

Mendel resumes his place at the table, and clears his throat. His eyes are focused on the paper.

Esteemed Mendel: I hope this letter finds you and your dear wife in the best of health. I received information from your cousin Bertha that my sister-in-law, Freda, and my daughter Fanny may be staying in your home. I pray that this is so, and I thank you for your hospitality.

"Don't stop, I can see there's more."

"Of course, dear." He clears his throat again and starts to speak.

Freda will tell you about the passing of her dear Avram. His sister Bertha is now the owner of their home.

Mendel glances at me and grins again. "Where was I?" He points to a line in the text. "Oh, yes.

Tell my daughter that she is to be obedient. She was to be married next year and left us without a word. I'm sure she is sorry. Now that she is in your care, I trust you to remind her of her place. Let her work hard to earn her keep.

Mendel keeps raising and lowering his eyes.

Perhaps in America, girls can attend school. This is not proper for a girl from our village. Under no circumstances is she to do this. She does not have my permission.

I can tell that he's making up this part of the letter. It doesn't even sound like Papa. Another throat clearing. Mendel looks very pleased with himself.

I know it's not true. "Let me look at it, please."

"What for? Your papa sent it to me." He returns the letter to the top drawer. His hands are no longer trembling. He locks it and pockets the key. He seems to relax, but Sophie's not through with him. "So, Mendel you knew everything and kept it from me. Now, we're stuck with them." She looks in our direction. "But not for long. You can stay here, for now, but get busy working. You, too, Fanny, forget about school. I'll expect two dollars this Friday and every week to come. And start saving for the day when you are no longer welcome here."

Sophie laughs. Her mood is changing. She serves herself a large portion of sardines and onions. She mops up some of the congealing oil with a slice of bread. I start to gag. Tears escape. My aunt excuses herself and escorts me to the washroom.

When we return, we head straight to our room and close the door. Aunt Freda takes a skirt from my satchel and her sewing kit from her sack. She threads a needle and begins to make a hem.

"What...?"

"I noticed the schoolgirls are wearing shorter lengths."

"But, Sophie said—"

"Listen, Fanny, you will go to school. I'm the one you can count on, remember?" I hug my aunt. I'm really tired. What an evening this has been. The last vision that appears before my drooping eyelids is the key.

$\mathcal{E}$ I G H T

Fitting In

$\mathcal{I}$'m up bright and early. I want to leave as soon as possible, before Sophie gives me a hard time. The skirt Aunt Freda hemmed is just right. I dress quickly, but I spend a few extra minutes fixing my hair. I comb through the top and sides several times. Then I tie it in the back with my new yellow ribbon. I admire my reflection in the window. "Auntie," I whisper, "I'm leaving."

She rubs her eyes open and stretches her arms above her head. "What time is it? Am I late?"

"Not at all. Sophie's not even up yet. I'll see you later, at the factory, and don't worry. I'll find it. I have my map." I hold out my notebook and then tuck it under my arm. The piece of paper the secretary gave me yesterday is in my pocket. I slip out quietly and close the door behind me.

Not a moment too soon. I hear her. "Freda, get up. Work today. Where is...?"

I run down the two flights of stairs and out to greet the rising sun. This is the first time that I can walk here without being surrounded by crowds. The streets are almost empty. I have no idea what time it is, but I do know the day. Today is Tuesday. The paper boys are out early, as well, shouting the latest news in English, Yiddish, and other tongues. Their first customers are the pushcart vendors, just beginning to set up. The news of the city and the world will come to them first. Right now, the only news that is important to me is that today is my day, the day I've wished for and waited for, my first school day.

I skip and then run across the cobblestones, following my personal map, made just for me. I remember the book of maps Papa had bought for Louie. It was large with so many colors and words, a world of words. One day, I'll buy one of those for myself. For now, my world is contained on one page of my copybook. I say the name of each street as I reach it, 'Orchard,' 'Allen,' and 'Eldridge.' I turn right. 'Grand,' 'Delancey,' and 'Rivington.'

The school is even bigger than I remembered. I'm here, at last, and...I am all alone. I climb the steep steps to the top. The huge doors have heavy padlocks hanging from their handles. Where is everybody? Isn't this the right school? Aren't they waiting for me? Is this a bad dream? Will I wake up, back in Vahivka, waiting for Louie to come home from his school, waiting for my wedding day?

I'm feeling dizzy. My right leg is full of pins and needles. I sit on the stairs and close my eyes. I think I hear the village bells. They're coming closer. How can that be? I look up to see a large man approaching. His blue work pants are held up by a thick leather belt. A bracelet-size ring of jangling keys is attached to his belt loop. He has heavy boots, but not the kind the cossacks wear. I should be scared, but his cheerful grin reminds me of David. And, when he speaks, he sounds like David, too.

"Moornin."

I don't know what he's saying.

"Aah, a noo girl." He points to me.

I shake my head. I show him the cover of my copybook, and I tell him my name. "Fanny Tatch."

Now, he points to himself. "Dennis Daly." He lifts the ring of keys and looks them over. There must be one hundred, maybe more. I'm thinking about the black metal key Mendel used to lock up Papa's letter. Maybe Dennis Daly has one just like it. The largest of the keys fits perfectly into the weighty padlock. He opens one of the massive doors just as the 'tai-ping' lady reaches us.

"Moornin, Miss." He tips his cap.

A blush of pink tinges her cheeks, and she offers a slight smile. Then she turns to me. "Urr-lee," she says. I show her my copybook and read my name aloud. "Fanny Tatch." I reach into my pocket and hand her the slip of paper. Evidently, it's my ticket in. She leads me to the office and points to the bench.

"Sit," she says. I remember. So I sit and wait. I've waited all these years for this day. I can wait a little longer. I keep busy while I'm waiting. I study. It's true that I've never been to school, but I've watched my brother at his books. I'd seen him read and reread each page. I heard him repeat his lessons to Papa in the study. I could hear the pride in Papa's voice. I was also proud of Louie...and envious of his right to attend school. Now that privilege will be mine as well. All those years of observing Louie at his task will be put to use. My copybook rests on my lap. I count the letters of my name, five and five—even, balanced. Good. I trace over each letter with my finger. I'm not using my pencil yet. If the point gets dull, I won't have anything to sharpen it with. After a while, I turn to the last page of my notebook, and I study the grid. I'm trying to memorize my map, so I can navigate the streets with my head up.

I think I hear my name. Yes, I do. Two times, with a loud squeaky voice. It's the secretary who gave me the paper yesterday. I didn't notice when she came in. I was studying. I stand. Her bony fingers grasp my elbow, and she leads me out of the office and down the hall. We pass a long row of classroom doors. I count them. We stop in front of the fifth one.

This door is partially open. I peek inside. A tall, slim woman stands in front of the room next to a large wooden table. Her back is as straight as the stick she holds in her right hand. She is pointing to a line of letters above the slate board. I recognize the shapes of the letters. They are the same as those in the countess's fashion magazine; the same as those on the street signs here in New York, and the same as the letters in my name, on my new copybook. I'm ready.

The secretary pokes my arm and pushes me inside. I am almost reminded of the photo of the American classroom. I am finally here. But there is a problem.

There are rows of small desks with attached seats. The boys and girls sitting in them fit perfectly. I will not. These children are even younger than Louie, maybe six years old. They are all repeating the letters as the teacher points to them, "eee-ef-gee..." They are learning the alphabet, just as Louie learned his *aleph-bet* so long ago, his first year at school. This must be the first grade. I am in the first grade. Of course.

The teacher's stick leaves the letters for a moment and indicates an empty desk at the rear of the room. I am poked again by the office lady, this time in the center of my back. I walk slowly to my new seat.

The pointer has returned to the top of the board, and the children continue reciting their letters, "jay-kay-el..." good. Now I can slip in quietly. I take a deep breath, in and then out. I bend my knees. I sit on the edge of the small seat and try to slide my legs under the little desk. My right knee squeezes in and is stuck. I don't know whether to try to pull it out or push harder. I try everything. I shove my leg to the right. It doesn't move. Then I push it forward. No luck. I take another deep breath and pull with all my might. My leg is released, and I fall flat on the floor. Hard. Just as the children reach the last letter, "zee," I scream out in pain, "Oy!"

The boys and girls turn at once, some pointing at me, all laughing. I can feel that familiar hard lump return to my throat. My chin is quivering. I do not want to cry my first day in school. I do not want to cry.

I look toward the window and pray for something. I don't know what. Maybe a larger desk, maybe a new class, maybe—*Bang, bang, bang*. The sound is coming from the front of the room. It's the teacher's trusty stick, demanding order. The children sit up in their seats and face the letters, again. "Copy," they are commanded. They open their notebooks and begin to write each letter. Pencils just like mine are held tight in their small hands.

I can hear her footsteps. The teacher reaches out, holds my left arm, and helps me to stand. She takes my notebook and reads my name, "Fanny Tatch." She leads me to the front of the room and pulls out her own chair. "Sit," she says. So I do. She shows me her name on the board, and says, "Miss Hall."

I don't know what to do next, so I open my copybook and begin to write the American alphabet, here in this American classroom. It's not exactly what I expected, but it's a start.

I am writing as neatly as I can. I copy the letters from beginning to end. I count them. Twenty-six. Then I write them again, even more carefully. I look them over. I am proud of my effort. I place my pencil inside and close my notebook.

I rest my arms and lean back in the teacher's roomy chair. I wonder what will happen to me when she wants to sit down. I look up. Most of the children are busy writing. Miss Hall is walking around the room, stopping every so often to look at a notebook or make a comment. I can't hear or understand her words, but her voice is gentle, and her manner is kind.

I hear a muffled sound. Someone is crying. Very quietly. It's hard to tell, but I am no stranger to tears. I spot a small boy with his head hidden in the crook of his left arm. A yellow pencil is gripped tight in his right hand, but he is not writing. He is seated in the second row, near the door. I look for the teacher. She is at the back of the room, leaning over another student's desk. I don't know what to do. The crying is a little louder now. He seems to be gasping for air and trying to stifle any sound. I know how it feels to hold back tears. It is painful.

Without thinking, I get up from Miss Hall's seat and tiptoe over to the boy. He is still hiding his head, but I can see perspiration dripping from his copper-colored curls. I use my hankie to wipe the back of his neck. He lifts his head and stares at me. His eyes are still wet and rimmed in red. They are an amazing shade of green. They remind me of one of the gemstones sewn into the seams of my aunt's vest. Beautiful. A shame to fill them with tears.

"Fanny," I say, pointing to my heart.

He sniffles, wipes his face with his sleeve, and points to himself. "Dan-nee," he mutters. He shows me the cover of his notebook. Someone wrote very neatly, "Danny." It's almost like Fanny. Only the first letter is different.

"Fanny, Danny," I say. He smiles. One tooth is missing. I remember Louie at his age.

I open Danny's copybook to the middle. It is half-filled with shaky writing. He holds up his pencil and shrugs. He's having trouble. I place my right hand lightly over his and guide him as he writes the letters. He says them clearly, and I try to repeat each one. Sometimes he nods his head, and sometimes he giggles at my pronunciation. I laugh a little, too. I don't even hear her coming.

Miss Hall taps my shoulder. She startles me. Maybe I'm doing the wrong thing. I don't want her to be angry with me. I take a few steps away from Danny's desk. The teacher is smiling.

The rest of the morning passes quickly. There are many things to observe and try to learn. I am back at Miss Hall's desk, copying something that the class had recited. They were all standing with their small hands over their hearts. It sounded nice, almost like singing or a prayer. I don't have any idea what it means, but I am writing the words. Carefully. Neatly. I want to do everything as well as I can. This is my chance. I hear a soft rumbling noise. I look over at Danny. He is writing, too, trying his best. That's all we can do. The noise is getting louder. It seems to surround me. Something is gnawing inside my belly. Oh, it's me. I'm hungry. Of course. I ran out early this morning without breakfast, whatever that would have been. I don't have anything for lunch, and then I have to go to work. On an empty stomach.

I wonder how Aunt Freda is doing at the factory. I hope Sophie isn't giving her a hard time. About me going to school and all. I wonder if Mike is there to help my aunt on her first day. I wonder if David will be there later. I want to show him my schoolwork. I wonder if Papa really said no school in his letter. I wonder how I can ever know. I wonder—

A bell pierces my thoughts. The students close their notebooks and stand. They walk to the front of the room and form two straight lines, in size order. Danny is in the middle of the boy's line. He is clutching a small grease-stained paper bag. The other children hold sacks of their own. Mmmm, lunch.

I don't know what to do, so I stand.

"No, Fanny, sit. Wait." Miss Hall pushes me gently back into her seat. She walks to the head of the line and leads the class out of the room, leaving me all alone...and wondering about everything.

My head is beginning to hurt, maybe from being so busy or from trying so hard. Maybe from hunger. Maybe from so much wondering. I can feel a tingling in my legs and feet. Maybe from sitting so long. I decide to walk around the room until the teacher returns. I wonder if she remembers she left me here.

As I pass the children's desks, I straighten their notebooks and pencils. There is a bookcase in the back of the room, crammed with a variety of volumes. I begin to organize them by thickness and colors. One orange-covered book drops to the floor and opens to the center. I kneel.

I see an illustration of a girl about my age. Her dark curls fall to her shoulders. Her eyes are round with wonder. One hand is placed on the lid of a box. Her fingers are reaching for the lock. There must be hundreds of words on the opposite page. I wonder if I'll ever be able to read them. I lean forward, and I stare at the girl for a while. She seems so real. I wonder what her name is.

"Pandora." My heart skips a beat. I look up. It's Miss Hall. She's smiling again. I didn't even hear her come in. I was lost...in this book.

Miss Hall picks up the book and hugs it to her chest as if it were an old friend. She holds a paper sack in her other hand. "Here, Fanny," she says and starts walking toward her desk. I try to get up, but I lose my balance and fall back. My legs shoot up in the air. I'm pulling my skirt down over my knees, when I hear heavy footsteps outside the room, and the sound of many keys.

I manage to get to my feet just in time to see Dennis Daly walk in, carrying a student desk, more my size, and a chair. Miss Hall leaves the Pandora book and the paper sack on her own table. She brings my copybook and pencil over to an empty spot near the rear of the room.

Dennis Daly places the furniture there and looks toward Miss Hall for approval.

"Thanks," she says and smiles at him.

Color rises in Dennis Daly's neck and face. He turns and heads out the door, his keys jingling all the way.

I'm pleased. Now I have a place to sit and learn. "Thanks," I say. I'm beginning to communicate in English. I feel happy and hopeful. I decide to copy more words from the board. I reach for my pencil and am startled by the rumbling noises coming from my stomach.

"Hungry, Fanny?" She pats her own belly. That's easy, *hungerik*.

"Hungry," I say and nod my head. Miss Hall's paper sack contains a cheese sandwich, a thin slice of yellow cheese on white bread. She takes one half for herself and hands the other part to me. Another chance for me to say thanks. And I mean it.

"You're welcome," she replies and returns to her desk to eat.

Now that my belly is not so empty, I begin to relax. My head feels so heavy that I lay it down gently on my new table. I have a vision of Papa in his study, nodding his head and smiling. I can see an outstretched hand, holding an open book. Louie is reading, I think. But, it's not his voice, I hear. It's mine. And the words are...English: sit, here, wait, thanks, you're welcome. Papa looks happy. He rises from his chair, reaches into his vest pocket, pulls out a honey-colored candy, and drops it into my hand. "Learning is sweet," he says and disappears just as a loud bell rings in my ear.

"Learning is sweet." That phrase resounds in my head all afternoon, as I join the children in copying numbers and more words. Words I don't know, not yet. "Learning is sweet." I last heard that from Reb, and now from Papa in a daydream. There's a connection. Reb is the key to Papa. *I've got to get that letter.*

I pop the honey candy in my mouth just before leaving school. Its sweetness reminds me that tomorrow will be another chance for learning, and it blocks out any worries about what awaits me at work. My eyes dart back and forth over my map, as the streets beneath my feet match those on paper. Amazing. Before I know it, I'm on Ludlow Street. I swallow the last bit of my candy and look up at the sign. "Ludlow Industries," I say to myself. The sweetness on my tongue is turning sour, and my feet are glued to the road.

Mama always said, "Look at the big picture." I know. This job is part of my picture now. So I straighten my spine, breathe in deeply, lift my right foot, and enter the noisy, busy building.

Here to greet me is another part of my picture, Sophie. "So you're finally here. Plenty for you to do." She shoves the handle of a huge broom into the center of my chest. My pencil falls out from my copybook and rolls into a pile of fabric scraps, pins and threads. "Good, you can leave it there. You've been to school, and now that's through. I'll need you here tomorrow morning, early." She kicks the pencil deeper into the pile and walks away. I can feel every eye on me. A knot forms in my throat and begins to grow.

Through a veil of tears, I see a blurry hand reach into the scrap pile to rescue my precious pencil. It's David, himself. I feel a warm blush rising from my neck. I lower my head and reach into my pocket for my hankie. My fingers trace the fine embroidery. Aunt Freda's work. Suddenly, I straighten up. I don't want to add to her troubles. I need to be brave. I swallow hard, several times, willing the lump to dissolve. I clear my throat. "Thank you, David," I say, in English, and I hold out my hand.

"Wait, Fanny." He dusts off the pencil with his own plain handkerchief, pulls out his folding knife, and brings back the nice sharp point. Sophie stomps over and tries to grab it from him. He's quicker than she is, by far. David runs up the stairs, waving the pencil in the air as he goes.

"Hmph...Nothing but trouble since you got to New York. Try to make yourself useful." She pokes me again with the broom handle.

I'm glad to have something to do. I move the broom from one end of the floor to the other, back and forth across the room. The droning of the machines has a certain rhythm. I walk to the beat, repeating today's lessons in my head. First the alphabet, then only the letters of my name. And Danny's name, I say as many English words as I can remember: wait, hungry, good, copy, sit, thanks, you're welcome...Pandora! And then I say them again. And again. The machines don't bother me at all, now. They're helping me to learn.

I keep sweeping, and the scraps keep falling. The girls and women work without a break. They only stop to rethread or pull out a jammed garment. Or when Sophie comes over to scold them. After a while, even these interruptions don't keep me from my thoughts. It's like I'm in another place. And working here, too. To the drone of the sewing machines. My mind keeps drifting back to the classroom, to my new desk, to the bookcase in the back of the room, to all those books, especially the one about Pandora. I'm about to enter her world, when the shriek of a whistle pulls me away. And then, silence.

I look up to see the women pushing back their chairs, rising and unfolding their bodies. Some are stretching their arms and shaking their legs. Others are hurrying to the door, anxious to get out. But not before Sophie checks and counts the stacks of their labor.

"Stop staring, little girl, and get back to your broom." So I sweep around the half-deserted expanse, not looking up. I am focusing on the mountains of scraps forming at my feet. I'm not recalling today's lessons, or drifting in and out of my classroom. It's too quiet, now. The only sounds I hear are chairs scraping and feet shuffling toward the light of the half-open door. And Sophie's counting. She begins in English, "One, two, three, four..." As the numbers get higher, she lapses into Yiddish. *"Tsvantsik, draysik, fertsik..."* All this counting with a measured, low voice, occasionally rising to a shriek, "So you think you've done forty blouses today. I see thirty good ones, and then these."

I can hear seams ripping, and buttons popping all over the floor. I glance sideways to see a hill of discarded garments next to the tally table. Mostly, the women do not respond to

Sophie's criticisms. Not directly. But the complaints appear in reddened cheeks, furrowed brows, and watery eyes. And in muffled utterances in a variety of tongues.

I can hear the impatient tapping of feet of those waiting in line to turn in their labor. And steady steps approaching. Mike appears, holding his ledger, one like Papa had in his store. He lets it fall open on the table in front of Sophie. His voice is quiet, but sure. "Shah! Sophie, *genug*. Enough of your scolding. Just count."

Mike bends over his notebook, writing tidy numbers next to each name. I guess this is how the workers get paid. Eyes are no longer on Sophie. The power has shifted to the man with the pencil.

Now that the rows are clear, I decide to lift each chair and place it on the table, like we did in school, before leaving. I didn't know why at the time, but now I do. It's for the sweeper! My broom starts moving to the memory of Dennis Daly's keys. Jingle, jangle, jingle...I'm back at school. That is, until I reach the end of the second line.

I run right into someone. I look up. It's Angela. She's having trouble gathering her garments. She tries to steady her shaky hands. The clothes keep slipping out of her trembling fingers. She backs away from the sewing machine as if it were her mortal enemy. This is not an easy job for her. I guess I'm really lucky to have just a broom to contend with. I lean it against a bench and lend a hand to Angela.

I can't sew, but I'm really good at folding fabrics. I was happy when Papa let me help him in his shop. It was a treat for me, being there; that is, until Reuben came along. I shake that thought out of my head, finish folding, and hand over the neat pile.

"*Grazie*, er, thanka you."

"You're welcome." I take a good look at her. Angela's timid smile reveals two cute dimples. She has shiny black hair. Her eyes are dark, too, but with shadows underneath. Her skin is pale, probably from being indoors all day. She is about my height, and as far as I can tell, just about my age. I wonder how she came to be here. I wonder if she ever went to school. I wonder—

"Fanny, stop bothering Angela, and get back to work!" I look over to the tally table to see Mike's pencil in the air. Sophie is glaring at us. They are waiting for the last seamstress to turn in her work.

NINE

MAKING FRIENDS

I sweep closer to the counting table to watch Angela present her garments. Sophie is about to toss one of them into the discard pile, when Mike looks up from his books. "Not so fast, let's have a look." He holds it up, runs his fingers over the seams, and adds another number to the total.

"You're much too easy on the workers. That's not really good for business, is it? I should have a talk with the boss one day." Sophie's smile looks almost like a threat. Mike turns toward Angela. "Twenty-eight! Better each day. Good evening." I hear a muffled sigh of relief and the gentle closing of the door. And then the screech of Sophie's chair, pushing away from the table, followed by her shrill voice, heading upward. "Fre-ee-da! Time to go."

Next, a quieter tone. It's from Mike. "Freda will stay. There's still more finishing work to be done."

"And no one else can do it?"

"She's the one I need. This is an important job."

"Oh, so one day here, and already she's a miracle worker." The color is draining from Sophie's cheeks, and they are taking on a green tinge. And now red. "I don't know what you're up to, Meyer Gutnick, but your day will come." She leans in close to Mike, causing a shadow to fall across his forehead. As if he could sense its presence, he wipes it away with the back of his hand.

"Good night, Sophie. You can expect Freda and Fanny home later."

"Much later and they can go to bed without dinner. I'm not running a restaurant, you know." The door slams behind her. I take a deep breath and return to my work.

Mike stays at the counter for a while, tallying the day's production. From time to time, I see him glance in my direction. I hope I'm doing a good job. Finally, he clears his throat and points to the door. Oh, my goodness, does he want me to leave? So, soon. "Ah, Fanny, so Sophie is your *relative*?"

"No, not exactly. She's Uncle Avram's cousin."

"Uncle Avram?"

"Aunt Freda's husband." Mike opens his mouth and closes it again. He looks at the staircase and then back at his ledger. "So where is this husband? Is he still in the old country?" I shake my head.

"No, Aunt Freda would never leave him."

"Your uncle is here in New York?"

I lean the broom against a chair and walk over to the counting table. The words start to tumble out. "No, not here, he's gone, you see. Uncle Avram was sick for a long time. Aunt Freda took good care of him. After the funeral, we sat shiva for one week, and we left Vahivka—secretly, of course. I didn't know what to do. I didn't want to leave Papa, but my stepmother, Ida, arranged a marriage for me with her nephew, Reuben. He's awful. And I really didn't want to get married, anyhow. I wanted to go to school like Louie. So, we left. Everything and everybody."

I feel a warm tear on my cheek. I don't even try to wipe it away. I can't stop talking. "For a while, I thought we'd never get to New York. So much trouble on the journey. First the cossacks attacked Alexius's wagon, and then we had difficulties getting tickets at the train station in Kiev. I met a countess, and when I tried to return her comb, the guard on the train began to paw at me."

A chill runs down my spine. "We almost got on the wrong ship, and there was a terrible storm at sea. When we finally arrived, the doctor poked my eye and tried to keep me from getting off." I pause for a second to catch my breath. "And now, after everything, Sophie—"

"I know. But you're here now. It's going to be all right."

"Finished, Fanny?" I was so busy with my story, I didn't even hear David come in, and I don't know what he's saying. I recognize my name, but not the other word. David is holding a large roll of rope, and he's grinning, as usual. I can't help smiling back. I wonder how much he heard. What's the matter with me? He doesn't understand Yiddish, and I certainly can't tell my tale in English. Not yet, anyhow.

Before I can get to it, David picks up my broom and sweeps it across the entire first floor. He pushes all the scraps together to form a giant hill. Next, he uses the end of the broom to divide this mound into three parts. He steps back a few paces to regard his work. I watch David pull out several larger fabric pieces and lay them out in front of his feet. Finally, he sweeps each of the three piles into a cloth, wraps it tight, and ties the bundles with rope.

He picks up one of the packets and rolls it around and around in his hands. He tosses it in the air and catches it. Next, he holds it up high and throws it into large barrel. David repeats these actions two more times, and then he turns to me and bows. "Finished!"

"Finished," I repeat. "Finished!" I understand. He's done his job. It's a good feeling. I remember when Mama and Manya and I were done with the day's chores, we'd all say *fartik* together and clap our hands, if we had any energy left. So, I clap three times for David's efforts. He bows again and asks me a question. Something about school. I understand that word, for sure. School!

"Good," I say, nodding my head. I open my notebook and show him what I've written. He studies every line, just as Papa used to do with Louie's class work.

"Good, Fanny!" His grin spreads out from ear to ear. I can feel the color rising in my cheeks again. I turn my head and look around the room. It's clean. And quiet. The machines are still. The chairs are empty. For now. I wonder what Angela is doing this evening. And the other women. Are they resting, or do they have work to do at home? Do they have to share an apartment with some mean relative?

"Here, Fanny." David hands me my notebook and my pencil and my broom. He points to the staircase. I guess I'm needed there now. I can't wait to see my aunt. It's been a long day, and my stomach is beginning to rumble. "Good night, Fanny. See you tomorrow, after school." David opens the factory door.

"Tomorrow... after school," I reply. And then, he's gone.

When I get to the top of the stairs, I see Aunt Freda and Mike, seated across from each other. Both are resting their elbows on the wide table between them. They are leaning forward, deep in quiet conversation. Their heads are almost touching. Almost. Somehow, they look like old friends. I tiptoe back down three steps before they can see me.

I rub my forehead. I'm confused. What am I thinking? Men and women can't be friends...not in the old country, anyhow. But wait a minute—this is not the old country. Maybe anything is possible. Look, I'm a schoolgirl now. And I have a friend, too. David. I picture him smiling into my copybook and later tossing the scrap bundles into the barrel. That reminds me that I still have work to do.

I walk back up the three steps, letting my broom bang against the banister. By this time, Mike is back at his own desk, and my aunt is making careful stitches around a buttonhole.

It doesn't take long to sweep upstairs. Just some fabric trimmings, pins and threads. I sweep one last time to make sure that nothing remains. The gatherings form a small pile. I reach in to retrieve the largest piece of material, and wrap everything up into a little package. I use a strip of cloth to tie it together. Now it's Mike who is clapping. For me. "You're a fast learner, Fanny. Good for you."

"A dank...thank you."

"Like I said, a fast learner. And I see that you're able to get around the streets already, too." I show him my map. He traces the lines with one finger. His paper cuffs are worn out after a day at his ledger. "You had better start home now. The city is not a safe place after dark." My stomach is making louder noises now. Mike reaches into his pocket and hands me a few coins. "Pay me back on Friday. Take your aunt for some dinner."

Shadows fall across my map as we follow David's pencil lines left onto Delancey Street, past Orchard, and onto Allen for supper. It doesn't take long, as the streets are not crowded at this hour. The pushcarts are gone, and there are only a few stragglers heading home—whatever home may be.

This is the place where we had lunch yesterday. Was it really yesterday? It seems so much longer. I am happy to see the same waiter, and I open my hand to show him the coins. He takes two of them, and tells me to learn the value of money here. Not everyone can be trusted.

The sweet tea slides down the back of my throat and warms my empty belly. We are served a hearty meal. Crispy whitefish, boiled potatoes, and cucumber salad. There is no conversation until dessert is presented. I cut the puffy cheese pastry in the middle, and wrap my half in a paper napkin for tomorrow's lunch. My aunt shares her portion with me, finishes her tea, and clears her throat.

"Let's talk before we get back to Sophie's apartment." She clears her throat again. I've never known my aunt to be nervous before. "I had a little chat with Mike before you came upstairs." I nod my head. "It seems that he's a widower. His wife passed away almost a year ago."

"Really! I wouldn't have thought it. Look at how he covers his cuffs, and how his shirts are nicely pressed. Just like Mama used to do for Papa, and then it was my job. Does he have a daughter at home?"

"No, Fanny, no children for them, same as for Avram and me. He's alone. And the shirts are cleaned and pressed in a small laundry run by people from China."

"And still he protects his sleeves."

"That's the way he is. A good man, I think." I tell her how he took Angela's side against Sophie.

"Mike said not to worry about Sophie. She's a bone in his throat, too. He said he'll help you to continue to go to school and work in the factory, too."

"He sounds like a friend, Auntie. Is that possible?"

"I think it is. We can't let good friends slip through our fingers. We need them."

Our waiter comes over with a small brown paper bag. "I forgot to give you bread with your dinner." I open the bag to find two plump challah rolls inside. I add my leftover cake to the sack and think about lunch tomorrow, and school. And Sophie. We'd better get started. I don't even know what time it is.

I wrap my shawl high around my neck, but it can't keep out the night's chilly air. The sun has been gone for quite a while. A restless wind is rustling the pages in my copybook. I'm struggling to read my map in the dim light of the tall gas lamps.

Their flickering flames bring me back to Vahivka on a Friday night, many years ago. Mama's Sabbath candles cast a warm glow on every dear face at the table. Papa is smiling as Louie recites the blessing over the freshly baked challah. Mama is serving chicken soup. The steam rises from

the ladle, moistening her rosy cheeks. Manya's new engagement ring sparkles with promise. I am walking in from the
kitchen, carrying a platter of potato pancakes. I made them
myself, with a little help from Mama. I offer the first one to
Papa. He pats me on the head and tells me that I am becoming a great cook. "We'll find a good husband for you, Fanny,"
he says. "You're next."

"*No*, I'm not!" I yell into the wind.

"What's the matter, Fanny?"

I look around me at the deserted New York streets.

"Oh, nothing, Auntie, it's been a long day."

She holds my hand, and together we step carefully onto
each slippery cobblestone, over puddles, around dark corners
and onto the street where we live, for now. A deep sigh escapes
from somewhere inside me. We're almost there. I can't wait to
rest my head on the pillow. My legs are getting heavier with
every step. Thank goodness the wind is behind us, nudging us
along, and whoosh! A strong gust blows out the flame on the
street's only lamppost and shoves me into a trash can. Some
smelly stuff pours out, but I can't see what it is. The pitch-black
night is hiding everything. Aunt Freda pulls me up. I can feel
her hand shaking under my elbow. I grab it and head in the direction of Sophie's stoop. I squint my eyes to see better. There
is no light around. Clouds cover the sliver of moon. I've heard
that when a person can't see, his other senses are sharper.

I hear footsteps coming closer, and I can smell…schnapps.
I can feel a whiskery face next to mine, and a gnarled hand
reaching into my vest pocket. The drunk mumbles something in English, I don't know what, but I recognize the
word "girl." I need help to get him off. I count for my aunt in
Yiddish. "*Eyns, tsvey, dray…*"

She understands. We gather our strength, and on three,
we push the drunk away from me. Aunt Freda thrusts an
elbow into his chest, and together, we shove him into the
street.

I can hear his raspy voice calling after us, muttering words I've never heard before. Not that we stop to listen. We quicken our steps. I can barely make out the numbers, but I have a feeling we've arrived. We pull ourselves up one stair at a time.

We're almost at the door, when something screeches and runs across my feet. I can smell him, and he can smell my leftovers. His paw reaches for my sack. I catch my breath. "Oh, no, cat. I need this more than you do. Scat!" I clutch the bag from the restaurant. It holds tomorrow's lunch. And tomorrow holds...hope for a better day. But first, we have to face our landlords.

We make one stop first. In order to rid ourselves of the street's varied odors. It must be really late, because there is no line outside the washroom. It seems as if everyone in the building is asleep. Hopefully, this will be true of our hosts.

No such luck. I can see a faint light creeping under the door. I turn the knob and let my aunt in first. Mendel is seated in his wife's chair, the one that faces the door. He points to our places. Two bowls of soup await us. They must be cold by now. A layer of congealed grease skims the top of each serving. My stomach churns, and I look away.

"Not good enough for you, little girl? Be glad we saved your dinner for you."

"No, thanks, Mendel. Fanny and I are tired and want to rest."

"So, you don't want supper? Fine, I'll tell Sophie not to bother with your food anymore." I hear the bed creaking, and Sophie clearing her throat.

Mendel glances at the partially closed bedroom door. "Remember, when it's time to pay your room and board on Friday, that you were offered. You'll give the full amount, regardless."

"Fine, Mendel, good night to you...and Sophie."

Another sound from the back room. Mendel takes a key from his pocket and twirls it around his finger. He points to the locked desk. "I'm thinking of writing to your papa, tomorrow, Fanny. What do you think I should tell him?" I don't turn around, and I don't respond. My forehead is beginning to throb.

"So, no answer. I guess Sophie will have to help me. She's already begun to fill me in. Let's see, going to school without permission, keeping company with the Irish boy, and Freda, staying late for whatever reason. Not to mention walking the streets at all hours of the night. Your father should know..."

He gives the key a final twirl and slips it back into his vest. He grins and heads for his room, leaving the slimy broth at the table. *Feh.*

We fold our clothes neatly and place them on top of our satchels. Aunt Freda is snoring gently in a minute. I close my eyes and let the pictures of today's adventures pass before me...and then I drift off, as well.

$\mathcal{T}$ E N

$\mathcal{S}$ omehow, I don't think Mendel ever wrote back to Papa. Every once in a while, he takes out the letter and an ink bottle. But I can tell by the way he held his pen that he's not a good writer. Maybe that is holding him back.

He probably received a basic education back in the old country. (Even that was denied to me and all girls there.) But I can see he is not a scholar like Papa. Yes, Mendel can read the newspaper and an occasional letter, but I never see him read a book. As a matter of fact, I've never seen any books in this apartment.

That is, until recently. I'm talking about *Pandora,* my book. It was a gift to me from Miss Hall, when she promoted me to the fifth grade! I had been working really hard, learning English. I paid careful attention in class and spent my lunch hour with Miss Hall, practicing conversation.

David helps me with my homework every evening at the factory. We've become good friends. And I review my lessons each night before bed, reciting them to my aunt and teaching her as well. Actually, Miss Hall says I will make an excellent teacher one day. I still spend my lunchtime in the first-grade classroom, tutoring little Danny and any other pupil who needs a hand.

Now that I'm in fifth grade, the children are closer to my size. Miss James says I won't be there for long. I'll be moving up again. She's amazed at my progress. She doesn't know that I work at a job several hours after school each day and stay out as long as possible to avoid unpleasant discussions at home. I just stay focused on learning as much as I can in school. This is my goal for now. Mama always said there was a time for everything.

I rise at dawn each morning and head out the door as quickly as possible. School seems like my real home now. I am greeted warmly by Dennis Daly. He tips his hat and asks how it feels to be the early bird. Now I understand most of his remarks, and I tell him I'm fine. I'm not so shy in English. I don't turn red when I receive compliments. The school principal came by one day when I was reading to Danny, and she told me I was a fine young lady and an asset to the school. I thanked her kindly and returned to my task. It feels good to be helpful. I look up the word "asset" in our class dictionary. It actually means help or blessing. I am saving up to buy a dictionary of my own. Imagine, a nice fat volume filled with wonderful words.

As for money, we're doing the best we can. We pay the room and board out of our Friday pay envelopes. We put aside money for our evening meals. We eat supper after work, but we don't linger. We remember that it's not pleasant to be out after dark.

Our few necessities are purchased from Reb, and we visit with him from time to time. I told him about Papa's letters, and he said he'd be glad to read them for me, and to write back. I can read English now, but not Yiddish, so I'll be happy to accept his help. In a way, Reb is a friend to us, as well.

And speaking of friends, they seem heaven-sent. Like Angela. Her name means angel in English, *der malakh* in

Yiddish. She doesn't know Yiddish. Her first language is Italian. It sounds very pretty when she speaks it to Carmela.

But she and I speak English with each other, more each day. We're both learning, even though she's not at school. Angela did attend classes for a while. That was before she took over her mama's job. Now she works all day and then goes home to help care for her mother. Angela says her mama is very sick.

I told her about my mama's illness and death, and she started to cry really hard. Aunt Freda got up to hug the girl and asked what the matter was. Good thing Sophie had gone home, and Angela was upstairs with us.

Sometimes Mike asks her to stay late to help out with the finishing work. She says she can use the overtime pay, and she is happy to be learning a new skill. My aunt says that Angela does fine work.

Angela likes to cook, too. Sometimes we tell each other about our favorite recipes, and now I'm able to write them down. I'm saving them for the day when I have a kitchen of my own. I'll enjoy trying them out. Angela has already made my noodle pudding. She told me that her mama liked it.

We never said anything to Sophie about Angela's mama, but maybe one of the other workers did. In any case, she might have noticed the worried look on Angela's face, and her red-rimmed eyes. None of that stops the constant criticism of the girl's sewing. Who could work well under such conditions? Aunt Freda never finds fault with my friend's finishing stitches. She is a patient teacher, encouraging her all the time, and showing her how to embroider, as well.

Yesterday, I burst into the factory waving my prize in the air. It was a book of short stories given to me by Miss James. I came in second in the class spelling contest. It isn't a new book, by any means. The edges of the binding are quite tattered, and there are ink smudges on some of the pages. Still, it is a treasure to me. The second book in my collection. I can't wait to share it.

I ignore Sophie's frown and run over to Angela's chair. Empty! My heart sinks into my stomach. I know what has happened. Tears begin to spill from my eyes. Sophie calls out to me. "Stop your bawling. That's life. She'll be back to work in a few days. In the meantime, get the broom, and start to earn your pay."

I don't reply. I need the few dollars in my envelope. So, I keep my head down and let my fury out as I sweep. I don't see him coming, and I bump right into David. He's forever in and out on errands for the factory. You never know when he'll appear. But no matter the hour, I am pleased to see him. He always finds the time to offer me homework help and praise for my accomplishments. And he always has that cheerful grin ready to light up the darkest day. That is, until recently. I've been noticing him biting his lower lip and staring into the distance from time to time.

"Take it easy, Fanny."

"Sorry. I wasn't looking. It's Angela..." Tears start to spill again.

"I know all about it." He glances over at the scowling Sophie.

"We'll talk later." David points upstairs.

As usual, Sophie leaves at five o'clock, after tallying the workers' garments. I finish my job downstairs and head up to see my aunt. She has a pile of clothes to finish and no one to help her. I am just beginning to sweep her work area when David walks over.

"Come along, Fanny, we're off to see Angela at the wake. Your auntie will go later with Mike, himself." My aunt nods her approval. What can I do? I brush myself off and walk out the door with David.

This is the first time the two of us are on our own. It seems strange, and yet a little exciting. I keep looking around to see who is watching. In our village back home, for sure there was always someone nearby to check on our comings and goings. Not that there is anything to be ashamed of. We are on our way to comfort a friend at a wake. I have no idea what that is.

I let David lead me through familiar streets, across a wide avenue, and onto blocks outside the margins of my handwritten map. We stop in front of a two-story brick building. An older woman is standing on the steps. She is dressed in black from head to toe. From her woven kerchief to her dark cotton stockings and laced-up black shoes, she looks like someone from the old country.

"Buona sera, signorina." It sounds like Italian. She looks at me, and then at David, and shakes her head. So a different old country, but the same judgmental ways. Some things remain constant. But I am changing. I don't even blush. I just nod politely and walk inside. I have to blink my eyes several times and wait to get accustomed to the dark. I can see a light coming from an open doorway halfway down the hall.

As we head in that direction, the overwhelming scent of flowers and melting wax makes me feel dizzy. Somehow, David notices and holds my elbow with one hand. With the other, he removes his cap. He leads me over to a vacant chair near the front and tells me to wait there.

The room is filled with mourners and visitors. They are embracing each other, crying, and shaking their heads in dismay. So, this is the wake. Just like sitting shiva, but with a big difference. This gathering is taking place before the burial, not after. How do I know? My eyes follow David as he approached the coffin. I watch him kneel in front of the open casket, make the sign of a cross over his heart, and clasp his hands in prayer.

Others following him do the same. I am wondering what I will do when it is my turn. I am also wondering what the people around me are saying, and who they are. And where is Angela?

David returns, takes my hand, and walks me over to the first row of seats. Angela stands up immediately and wraps her arms around me. We both sob the tears of motherless children. A man stands up and pats my friend's back.

"Fanny, this is my papa."

Her father's eyes are wet, too. He keeps fussing with his shirt collar. He opens and closes the buttons of an ill-fitting suit. He presses my hand between both of his. They are rough, from years of hard work, I'm sure. Then, without a word, he falls back into a chair and stares at the chest containing his wife's lifeless body.

It takes me back to Papa, as they lowered Mama's coffin into the ground. He was the first to toss a shovelful of earth onto the lid of the simple pine box, as was the custom. As the others took their turn in this ritual, the rabbi chanted, "May Shira go to her place in peace." And Papa collapsed. It took him a full year to overcome his grief and try to build a new life with Ida. Maybe he regrets that decision.

I start to think about him and Louie and when I would see them again. And Ida, too, I suppose. I know I need to get in touch with them. Reb said he'll help, but how can I get my hands on Papa's letter?

My thoughts are interrupted by Angela's voice. She is introducing me to her brother, Sergio, and three younger sisters. Then several aunts, uncles, and many cousins. They all hug me in turn, calling me *buona amica*.

"Good friend," Angela tells me, and she accompanies me to view her mama. A woman is kneeling at the casket. She stands and motions for me to take her place. I hesitate. Angela puts one arm around my shoulder. "It's all right, Fanny, different ways, same feeling." She taps her heart.

"What was your mama's name?" I asked her.

"Carmina. It means song."

Just like Shira, I think. Pretty names with the same meaning. It is so sad that both left this world before they had finished singing.

I take a good look at Angela's mother. She is wearing a lovely blue dress. Pink roses are embroidered on the collar. They look familiar. I glance at Angela. She nods her head. I know where she learned those stitches. Aunt Freda is a good teacher. Carmina's cheeks are tinted the same color as the flowers, but they are hollow. You could see she had suffered, like Mama. A chain of pearls is entwined around her thin, stiff fingers, and a golden cross falls across the pleats in her dress.

People are waiting to pray over her. I can hear others entering the candle-lit room. I bend my knees for just a moment and whisper close to her ear, "May Carmina go to her place in peace." Angela waves to David and takes my hand again. "I'll be back at work in two days, Fanny, on Thursday." Before I can answer, she is pulled into the arms of a new arrival. It is time to leave.

The plan was for us to wait for Mike and Aunt Freda at our usual restaurant, the one where David took us on the day he helped me register for school. Mama always said that life is a circle. That saying was about to prove itself again.

We order soup and David's favorite, potato knishes. I didn't realize how hungry I was until the food arrives. I eat quickly and gulp down my tea. Not David. He keeps looking around the large room, tapping his foot, and clearing his throat. Finally, he speaks. "Let's have a look at what you learned in school today."

He thumbs through several pages of my notebook. It is a bigger one now that I have been promoted to a higher grade. His hand is shaking. He stops at the poem I'd copied in class. "Ah, good writing, Fanny, let me hear you read it to me." The cheerful grin returns for a moment.

I glance around to see if anyone is looking at me. No. Not really. The tables are filled with people, mostly resting a bit after a hard day's work. Some are having the only square meal in their day, like me. Many are lost in their own thoughts, while others engage in animated conversations. I don't want to call attention to myself. But David is waiting, so I lower my voice, and begin to recite the lovely poem, written by William Wordsworth.

> *I wandered lonely as a cloud*
> *that floats on high o'er vales and hills,*
> *When all at once I saw a crowd,*
> *A host, of golden daffodils;*
> *Beside the lake, beneath the trees,*
> *Fluttering and dancing in the breeze.*

I had thought to share this with my aunt first. I wanted her to draw a picture on the page, like the one in school, of the lively yellow flowers. But David is the perfect audience. He has the same proud look that appeared on Papa's face when Louie recited his lessons. And then, something else. Tears begin to well up in his eyes. Before I can ask him why, he reaches across the table and takes both of my hands in his. "You're doing great, Fanny. It's been a pleasure to follow your progress. You must write to me from time to time and let me know what you've been learning."

"What are you talking about?"

David doesn't answer. He opens my notebook to the back page, takes my pencil, and begins to copy some lines from a scrap of paper.

"What are you doing? What's happening?" My voice is rising, and I can feel people were turning away from their own activities to watch us. I don't care about them. David keeps at his task, pressing harder and harder, as he writes. Too hard. The pencil's point snaps and jumps off the table. David uses his pocketknife to sharpen it, as he has done so many times since the day we first met. He places the pencil in front of me, along with his penknife.

"Keep it, Fanny, you'll be needing to do this yourself from now on."

I just keep staring at him. I don't know what to think or to say, so I retreat into my old habit of keeping still. Then he pushes over my copybook and points to his own writing.

"This is where I'll be going. I'll be taking the train early tomorrow morning." What train? To where? The questions stay in my head. I can't speak, so I try to make out what David has written. It looks like a jumble of letters and numbers on the page. I sound out "Chi-ca-go." I said it again, "Chicago. I don't know that word, David. What does it mean?" I think I should get a dictionary soon.

"It's a place, Fanny, a city where I'll be living with me mum. She and me sister are heading there from Ireland. Katie's husband, Brendan, has family in Chicago, and they got a steady job for him there. And one for me, too. With good pay. It's hard to leave New York. It's been my home for four years...and you, Fanny, especially you."

I start to blush. I hope I'm not going backward—back to being so shy.

"Wouldn't it be great to take you along with me?" He looks up at the ceiling. "But the timing's off. Your plans and dreams are here, aren't they? Just keep going, Fanny, and growing into the wonderful woman you're becoming, and maybe one day..."

I hear footsteps approaching our table. Mike and my aunt are arriving after the wake. I don't look up right away. I close my notebook, slipping my pencil and David's knife into the middle. The waiter comes over to take their order and to bring more tea.

"Are you all right, Fanny?" asks Mike. Aunt Freda studies my face and then turns her gaze toward Mike. I see her poke his ribs with one finger. "Redn nisht." I wonder what she told him not to say. And then it becomes clear. They already know about David's move. That must be why they gave us time to be together. For a private good-bye, of a sort.

Not much more is said that evening. Aunt Freda takes one last sip of tea, stands up, and goes over to David. She gives him a big hug and wishes him all life's best. He rewards her with his famous smile and hugs her back.

"Thanks, Auntie. Fanny's got my new address in Chicago. I'll be waiting for a visit. Bring Mike along, too." He winks.

Mike pushes back his chair. He shakes hands with David and thanks him for being such a good helper. He walks with us up to the corner of Orchard and Grand Streets. That's where my aunt stops. She tells Mike that we'll go the rest of the way on our own.

"Let me take you to your door."

"No, Sophie will have something to say about us being out together. I don't want to get her started."

"Oh, don't pay any attention to her talk. She likes to make herself seem more important than she is. The boss will be at the factory on Friday. Sophie's been saving up some complaints about me. Mr. Blum knows who to trust."

A shadow of doubt crosses my aunt's brow. "Don't worry *mayn tayer*. It will be fine."

She waves him away, and we continue walking toward Hester Street. Did I hear Mike say, "my dear" to Aunt Freda? Really?

I wake up exhausted this morning. I'm having trouble getting out of bed. My legs are cramped up from riding the rails all night. Last night's dream had me sitting in one of the cars, looking out the window. I was trying to read the signs at each station, but I didn't recognize the letters. The train went faster and faster, never stopping. I looked around me. I was the only one in the wagon. When the ticket collector finally arrived, I asked him where we were headed. He answered me in a language I'd never heard before and held out his hand. All I had was my notebook. When I showed it to him, he called out, and the conductor appeared. They spoke with each other in their strange tongue and nodded their heads.

Before I knew it, we made a sudden turn, throwing my copybook up in the air. I kept trying to retrieve it, but the train's speed tossed it all around. I was at my wit's end, running from one side of the car to the other, falling over the empty seats. Tears streamed down my cheeks and onto my rumpled cape. I called out for someone to help me. No one came. I sat down on the floor, and let my head sink down into my lap. I had given up hope.

Hope. That's what Pandora had left in her box, after all the bad things had escaped. Hope, I thought. I hope...The train was slowing down and pulling into a station. I lifted my head and pulled myself up. The porter handed me my notebook. "Here we are," he said in English. The doors opened. The letters on the station sign were as clear as day: New York. This is what I hoped for.

I force my legs to move, and I head off to the washroom. I want to wash the dream away and get on with my day, if I can. One person is up ahead of me. It's Sarah. "I've been looking for you, Fanny. I have something to tell you. I haven't seen you for so long."

"We come home late every evening. We eat out after work."

"I don't blame you." She looked at me. "Are you still in school?"

"Yes, I can read, now...and write."

"Good, Fanny, so you'll send me a letter sometime. My brother's son is in school, too. He can read it and tell me what it says...I'm leaving tomorrow. To live in Philadelphia. Maybe you'll visit me one day." Sarah takes an envelope out of her apron pocket. I can see a train ticket tucked inside. She tears off the corner where the name and address are written and hands it to me. I hug her. "Keep learning, Fanny, don't let anyone stop you. *Zay gezunt*." Another good-bye.

The morning passes quickly. I'm learning new things every day, and that makes me happy. More to write in my notebook and review every evening. More things to think about. To fill my mind. So I don't have time to dwell on changes, on unhappy news.

Right after the dismissal bell, I get a chance to ask Miss James about Chicago. She shows me a large book filled with maps. Something like Papa gave Louie so long ago. It's called an atlas. It says so right on the cover. And that's what Miss James tells me, too. Atlas. I like the sound of the word. It sounds like "at last" (*at last* I'm in school) or "at least" (I'm not happy in Sophie's apartment, but *at least* I have a place to sleep at night). I like to think about words. Some are friendly, and others are scary...sort of like people, in a way.

My teacher's finger traces a jagged line from New York, heading west to the city of Chicago. It's not far on paper, but to me, it's a world away. Then she shows me Philadelphia. A little closer. On another page of the book, we find maps of cities in Europe. Then, we look at a map of Russia and the Ukraine. Vahivka is nowhere to be found. Not here, anyway. But it exists. I should know. I lived there, and I left. And Papa is there, and Louie...and Ida.

A second bell rings, and I look up at the clock. Oh, my goodness. Where did the time go? It's half past three. I'll be late for work. I thank Miss James and run out the door.

Sophie greets me with her usual frown and some harsh words. "So what have you been up to now, Missy? Too smart to arrive here on time?" She shoves the broom handle at me. "I may not have the schooling to write it down, but it's all up here." She taps her head with her stubby forefinger.

"I'm saving up all this behavior to tell Mr. Blum on Friday. I'll have plenty to say. Not only about you, my little scholar, but about your precious aunt and her dear bookkeeper." Sophie glances upstairs and then gives me a shove. I start to sweep as faraway from her as I can. I bump into Angela's empty chair. Oh, my dear friend. I know what she's going through. I lower my eyes and let one lonely tear fall into the scrap pile.

I hear the door open and close, and footsteps. My heart stops. Can it be? I turn my head. No, of course, it's not David... it's a boy I've never seen before. A skinny one, younger than I am by a few years, I'd say.

"Stop staring at Fanny, and help her with the bundles. Then come over here. I have an errand for you. Remember who you work for, Hershel. I'm the one who got you the job. You should be loyal, not like some people."

Hershel backs away from Sophie and steps right into the middle of the scrap pile. He trips over his own feet, trying to get out of it, and wipes his forehead with the back of his sleeve. He's sweating. I recall my first day at the job, and I remember to be kind. I put my hand on his shoulder. I can feel him trembling under my fingers. Poor boy. He should be in school, like Louie. Hershel sends me a half smile. He does an adequate job of tying up the bundles, and he laughs out loud when I toss them into the barrel. Sophie looks over in his direction. "You are here to do a job, not to enjoy yourself. That's why it's called 'work,' and not 'fun.' We just got rid of one cheerful person. That was enough for me."

A picture of David's wide grin flashes before me. I miss David. I work in silence, but the voice in my head keeps repeating the first line in William Wordsworth's poem, 'I wander lonely as a cloud.' Over and over, 'I wander lonely as a cloud.'

Mike joins us for supper. We're all in a gloomy mood. Aunt Freda doesn't even protest when he escorts us right up to our door.

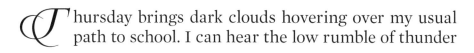

Thursday brings dark clouds hovering over my usual path to school. I can hear the low rumble of thunder in the distance all morning long. When the lunch bell rings, I head over to Miss Hall's classroom to tutor Danny. I'm so proud of the progress he's made. His handwriting is steady, and he's reading most words. He'll be promoted to second grade when school lets out next week. Just before he leaves for recess, Danny hands me a folded note. He giggles and runs out the door. I open it. Every letter is printed with care. The words are surrounded by the outline of a lopsided heart. He has written, "I love you, Fanny." Tears well up in my eyes, and I wipe them away with my hankie. More take their place, and I wipe them again. I can't seem to stop the flow. I hear Miss Hall approaching. I try to hide my face, but she puts one finger under my chin and turns my head in her direction. "What's the matter, Fanny?"

"Nothing."

"Then why the tears?" I don't know how to answer her, so I hold out Danny's declaration. "That's very touching, but what's really troubling you?"

"A friend from work...a very special friend...moved away to Chicago." I can feel another burst of tears. I wish they would stop. I gasp for more air and try to continue. "Chicago is very far from New York. I saw it in Miss James's map book..."

"I know, Fanny, missing someone is painful." She lowers her eyelids for a moment and takes out her own plain handkerchief. Then she straightens her back and points to her rolltop desk. It is a larger version of Mendel's bureau.

"I was saving this for next week. It's a gift from me in appreciation for all the help you've given to my students, and also...because Miss James will be promoting you to the eighth grade! After that, there will be four years of high school for you, Fanny, and whatever else you wish to pursue." She looks at me with the pride of a parent. Then she busies herself trying to open the lock on her desk. She pushes the key into the hole and rotates it back and forth. I can hear little clicks, but it will not open. Sometimes the person you need appears at just the right time. I can hear him coming. That is, I hear that jingling sound.

Dennis Daly tries almost every key on his huge ring. No luck.

"Please, Dennis, Fanny's gift is inside, and I'd like her to have it now." Miss Hall's smile turns into a grimace when her helper reaches deep into the back pocket of his overalls, and pulls out a...pocketknife! It's almost the same as David's, the one I have hidden in the bottom of my satchel, under the bed, in our room, in Sophie's apartment. I watch in amazement as Dennis inserts the point of the shiny blade straight into the center of the keyhole. He gives it one strong twist to the right. This time I hear a loud click.

The desktop is unrolled to reveal an assortment of items. Among them I spot a small stack of books with leather bindings, a faded photo of a family, framed in silver, and a porcelain mug decorated with yellow flowers and golden script, spelling out what might be her name, Flora. Lovely to have such treasures. I could stand here all day studying them. That is, if time would stand still, and the bells would stop ringing.

Lunch hour is over. Miss Hall hands me a solid package before dashing out of the room to collect her students from the schoolyard. And I am left, standing there, staring at my gift. It is wrapped with shiny cream-colored paper and tied with a yellow ribbon.

Dennis Daly's knife blade is snapped into place and returned to his back pocket. "Well, Miss Fanny, are we going to get a look at your present?"

Why not? I think, and I loosen the cord. I pull back the wrapping and catch my breath. It's a book of maps, an atlas. It says so right on the cover. I open it with care. There is an inscription on the first page. I recognize Miss Hall's graceful penmanship. *For Fanny, with thanks and all good wishes for your future. Follow your dreams, wherever they lead you.*

Fondly, Flora Hall. I thumb through a few pages of maps and hold each one up for Dennis to view. The second bell reminds me to return to Miss James's room. I fold the pretty paper around my precious book and head out the door.

A few dim rays of sunshine are peeking through the cloudy sky. Things are looking a little better than they did this morning. I'm almost skipping on my way to work. I can't wait to tell Aunt Freda about my promotion to eighth grade and show her my lovely atlas. And I'll see my friend. I've missed her.

Oh, no! Her chair is still empty. Angela said she'd be back today. I hope she's not ill. I can feel my brow wrinkling with worry. I'm standing still, staring at the vacant seat. I can't seem to budge. But not for long. A fist is pushed into the middle of my back. "Get moving, girl. You're here to work." Sophie hands me my broom, and I force my feet to find their rhythm. But I keep glancing at Angela's silent sewing machine.

"Don't bother looking over there. Your dear friend will not be there today or any other day. Whoever takes her place will be a great improvement. That's for sure."

I can hear Sophie's mocking laughter. I feel like my head is going to explode. I don't want to cry in front of her, so I sweep my way across the room. I almost fall over Hershel. He puts his finger over his lips.

"Shush, Fanny, Angela's upstairs, working with your aunt."

"Really, how did that happen?"

Then Sophie shoves him out of the way and comes really close to me. "You've said enough, Hershel. If you want to get along with me, you'd better learn to mind your own business." Her face is flame red. I can feel her hot breath on my neck.

"And for your information, Missy, somehow your darling aunt has persuaded Meyer to let Angela become a full-time finisher. Upstairs, and for more pay. Freda should be helping our own people, like I do."

Now, I'm mad. I don't address her by name, but I look directly into her eyes. "Anyone who is good and caring is my kind of people, and I don't care where they come from," I tell her. Now her face is the color of the beets I used to use to make borsht. She stomps back to the counting table. I can hear some of the machines slowing down. The workers are staring at Sophie and at me.

"Get back to work, before I replace the lot of you. You see what happens when a girl goes to school. She fills her head with all kinds of ideas and forgets her place."

That's the point, I think. *I never wanted to be in that place, the one chosen for me. I want to find my own place. Miss Hall said I can do that. I think I'm on my way.*

Eleven

A Fight in the Night

Aunt Freda and I take Angela to supper with us to celebrate her new position. Then we walk with her all the way to her apartment. We are not in any hurry to return to Sophie's place, but we know, sooner or later, we'll have to deal with another of her angry fits. As soon as we get there, my aunt hands her the weekly rent. It's not due until tomorrow, our usual payday, but we have enough saved. We think this will help to serve as a distraction. Sophie counts the money, slowly, biting her lower lip all the while. Finally, she speaks. "This is not enough, Freda."

"Of course it is. It's the same amount I've been giving every Friday."

"True, but that was then. This is now. Things change, don't they? Like at the factory. You took one of my workers upstairs with you. Since you're so important, it shouldn't be a problem to add another dollar a week, starting tonight." Sophie puts out her hand.

My aunt shakes her head. "We pay you more than enough. We're no bother to you. All we do is sleep here. A lot of our earnings go toward our meals."

"That's your choice, not mine. I'm waiting for the rest." Aunt Freda shrugs and takes a dollar bill from a pocket hidden deep inside her vest. She carries our meager savings with her all the time. Sophie doesn't even wait for the money to be offered. She grabs it without a thank you of any kind.

At that precise moment, everything seems to change. Thunder booms and a streak of lightning crashes against the window. The small hairs on my arms begin to rise. A chill runs down my spine, even though the air in the apartment is hot and stuffy. Sophie breaks the uneasy silence by calling out in the direction of her bedroom, "Come out, Mendel, and open the desk. The factory *k'nacker* just paid the rent, and I need to keep it safe."

My aunt throws both hands up in the air and lets them drop to her sides. Her voice starts low and rises gradually to a high pitch. "I'm not a big shot, Sophie; I work hard, just like anyone else there. And about Angela, you were never happy with her, anyhow. She's a good hand sewer, and we can use her upstairs. Why should that matter to you?"

"It matters a lot. Thanks to me, you and Fanny have good jobs and a roof over your heads. You should be grateful. Instead, you practically ignore us; you go around making friends with all kinds of people. You send your niece to school, where she's learning things she'll never need to know, I'm sure. It's not natural. My life turned out just fine without any schooling." Sophie sniffs a few times. It looks like she's trying to hold back her tears. But she doesn't cry. She takes a breath and continues her rant. "And if you're so unhappy here, take a good look around this neighborhood. People are glad to pay much more than you do to share a room with four others or sleep on a cot in someone's kitchen, believe me."

My aunt stiffens and feels in her pocket to check on our dwindling savings. "Maybe I *will* look around. Perhaps Mike knows of something..."

Sophie is turning red, again. Her cheeks are all puffed up. "Fine, Freda," she sputters. "But you'd better make it fast. As a matter of fact, why don't you leave tomorrow, bright and early, out the door. And good riddance."

"What are you saying, Sophie?" It's Mendel, just coming out of his room, in his pajamas, key in hand.

Sophie turns to face him. "You heard me. I've had enough of them. I wish I didn't have to see them at work, either."

"But, Sophie, we need their rent money, and after all, they're your relatives."

"We're not really related, and not anymore, for sure. Avram was my cousin, and now he's gone." She raises her eyes to the ceiling and lowers them to glare at me and my aunt. "They're nothing to me, and the sooner they leave, the better. Don't worry, Mendel, we'll get someone who'll be happy to pay us for the room, maybe even more money. You can ask around at your job. Boats are arriving from the old country several times a day. There are thousands of people who need somewhere to stay. Fanny and Freda will be gone in the morning, and you can find new boarders to move in by evening."

Sophie grabs the key from him. Her husband stands there, as if in a trance. The desktop lets out a few squeaks as it rises. I watch as our hard-earned cash is deposited into a small metal box.

I find my voice. "Why are you keeping our money, if you're throwing us out? Give it back!"

Sophie slams the roll top down, causing it to scream out in pain. Something white flutters to the floor. That puts Mendel into action. He bends down, plucks up the paper, and tries to stuff it into his pajama top. But he's not quick enough. Sophie pulls the page away from him and holds it out in front of her. I take a better look. My mouth opens, but no words come out. The red wax stamp that seals the envelope is still intact. My aunt must recognize it, too. "Redn nisht, Fanny."

She mouths the words. I wouldn't know what to say, anyway. They certainly won't give it to me...or the money that belongs to us. Sophie waves my papa's letter in the air.

"What's this, Mendel?"

"Oh, it's just—it's from a cousin...in Russia. You don't know him." Sophie stares in vain at the return address.

"Well, why didn't you open it?"

"I only received it yesterday. I didn't have a chance..." Mendel is fumbling with the buttons on his pajamas. One of them pops off and lands at Sophie's feet. He bends over to retrieve it and recaptures Papa's letter on his way up. Mendel rushes over to the desk, opens it halfway, and shoves the envelope inside. Then he turns the key and checks to make sure it is securely locked. This time, Sophie grabs the key.

"What else are you hiding?"

"Nothing, dear...just waiting to read the letter together when we have the time."

Sophie nods her head. "All right, Mendel, I hope it's not that your relatives are coming with many mouths to feed and little or no money to pay us. Maybe they'll expect to stay here for free. We'd better get new boarders fast, so we can tell your cousins we don't have room." She scratches her head. "Yes, I have it. We'll wait to read the letter until after the new people move in." Sophie is speaking to her husband as if we were already gone. Lightning flashes across their faces, and thunder continues to rumble, as we head to our room for the very last time.

We set out our clothes for tomorrow and slip into our nightgowns. I lay my head down on the flat pillow and stare at the ceiling. My eyes follow a long jagged crack just above the bed. It looks like a path, leading to nowhere.

My head is starting to ache, and I feel that familiar lump forming in the back of my throat. Rain beats against the windowpane, and tears wet my pillowcase. Aunt Freda's hand is on my shoulder. Her voice is calm and soothing.

"Don't worry, Fanny. We'll be all right. Try to rest. We'll get up nice and early. We'll arrive at the factory before Sophie does and leave our belongings with Mike. He'll help us to find a good place. It will be fine. Let's close our eyes."

So I try, but sleep doesn't come. Something is bothering me. Actually, two things: Papa's letters, one opened and one not. I need to get them. I must know what they say. I'll have to find a way to get in touch with Papa. So he'll know where we are, wherever that will be.

Aunt Freda is snoring away. I perk up my ears. The storm has subsided. A gentle breeze is rustling the leaves outside. I tiptoe out of bed in my bare feet, reach into my satchel, and open our bedroom door. It's dark and quiet in the hallway. I can't see a thing, but I can hear deep steady breathing from Sophie's room. Good.

I feel my way over to Mendel's desk. The floor boards creak with every step. My hand touches side of the bureau, and my pointer finger finds its way over to the keyhole. I thrust the tip of David's pocketknife right into the center, just as Dennis Daly did, and I turn it in the same way. The click is strong and certain. Did anyone else hear that? What should I do? I can't stop now. I've got to work fast. I lift the roll top only halfway. It lets out a squeaky protest. "Shah," I whisper to the desk as I bend over to peek inside. No luck. Everything is a dark blur. I push my hand into the opening. I feel through a pile of papers. The sharp edge of one makes a sliver of a cut on my thumb. It smarts, but I continue my search. I'm beginning to sweat. My knuckles hit something made of metal. It's cold to the touch and hard. It must be their money box. Our cash is in there. I should take it back—it belongs to us. I finger the lid, and I stop.

There's not enough time. I'm not in here for the money. Papa's letters are much more valuable to me. Back to the papers. I find an envelope. I turn it over, feeling both sides for the impression of Papa's initials. No, not there. I move my hand around. After several tries, I locate the one that has been opened. I hold it in my left hand, along with the folding knife. It takes a few more nervous minutes to locate the new letter. A chill runs down my spine as I run my fingers across the familiar wax stamp. I lower the desktop with the greatest of care. It stops just before reaching the bottom. I give it a little push. It's stuck. What should I do? I don't want them to notice that it's been opened, so I try again. The roll top moves an inch. It whines. I look around. Nobody. One more time, now a squeal. Almost there.

Suddenly, a light appears. It's shining in my eyes. I'm blinded for a moment. I try to hide the letters under my nightgown, and the knife slips out of my fingers. It clangs onto the floor. Mendel lowers his candle to see what it is. He jumps back as if he's seen a mouse. I bend to retrieve David's gift to me.

"Oh, no...she's got a knife! And my desk is unlocked. Drop that knife, Fanny, and give me back my money!" He's screaming.

"What's going on? Fanny, what's the matter?" Aunt Freda appears at the same moment as Sophie.

"I'll tell you what the matter is, Freda!" Sophie points her candle in the direction of the partially opened desktop and then onto my knife blade. "It's your niece! She's a thief and a criminal! Mendel, get the police. Hurry, she's going to kill us!"

"I'm not going out in the middle of the night. It's pitch black out there, and there are all kinds of troublemakers in the streets at this hour."

Sophie is starting to tremble. "Don't be a fool, Mendel, we have the trouble right here. Get the police, now!"

Mendel puts both hands over his ears and shakes his head from side to side.

Sophie scrambles over to where he's standing and yanks at his arms. Then she reaches up and yells into his ear. "You're a coward, Mendel. I'll have to take over."

He dashes back to his room. Something slams, and a lock turns. Sophie's eyes shift back and forth between the closed door and my knife. "Mendel is worthless, but I'm not afraid of you." She's pointing her finger at me. "I'll see that you're arrested and sent to jail. You didn't like the meals here. Wait till you see what's offered to you in prison. Ha! It's not a classroom, you know. And the other inmates are not exactly schoolgirls with ribbons in their hair. You'll be in there with other thieves, and even murderers."

"But, Sophie—" I try to interrupt her to tell her I was just trying to get Papa's mail, that I would never harm them. But she's not paying any attention to me. She's shaking all over and spitting out her words.

"As soon as it's light, I'll head off to the police station. But you won't be here. I don't want you in my home for even one more minute. Get out, now!"

Sophie is shrieking. Now I cover my ears. Mendel emerges from his hiding place. He's holding his pocket watch. "You can't send them out in the middle of the night. It's three o'clock in the morning. A few more hours, and they'll be gone." He turns to me. He's speaking quietly and slowly, as if to a very small child. "Be a good girl, Fanny. Hand over the weapon and return whatever you've taken from us."

I run to my room and bury the knife and Papa's letters deep in my carrying case. I can hear Sophie from here.

"I want them out now! You hear me? Now, or I'll start to scream into the streets. The police will hear me. Freda, get your crazy niece and leave, immediately!"

"But, Sophie, it's *finster* out there."

"The darkness shouldn't be a problem for you. Fanny found her way into our locked desk without any light. I want you out now, this minute. Go!"

I can hear a window opening. My aunt rushes into our room. She's as pale as a ghost. Her head is down. "We've got to leave now, Fanny. There's no other choice. Get dressed."

I feel faint. I lie down on the bed. A cold sweat breaks out on my forehead. Aunt Freda sits next to me, wipes my brow, and whispers in my ear. "I'm scared, too, Fanny, but what can we do? We'll stay in the washroom or the downstairs hallway until dawn. Then we're off to the factory. Mike will help, for sure."

I'm half-dressed when Sophie marches into our room. She stands by the door, feet apart and both hands on her wide hips. She begins to bark out orders.

"You will not stay in this building. I'll have the police here in a minute, and if you dare to go to the job, you'll find them there, waiting to take you away, Fanny. And Freda, as for your precious Meyer, he may not be in a position to help anyone. Mr. Blum will be back in the morning, and I have plenty to tell him. Your dear bookkeeper may find himself out on the street, too."

My aunt gasps. She shoves Sophie out of the way, and pulls me along with her. My blouse is still not buttoned, and my nightgown is hanging out the side of my satchel. We stop to use the washroom before heading down the stairs and out into the starless night.

Aunt Freda wraps a shawl around my shoulders and fastens her own cape. The storm has left a chill in the air and a myriad of puddles. I try to avoid them, but there is no light to guide my step. And I don't know where to go. But we must leave quickly. We can't stay here. Nor can we go to the factory. The police might be looking for us there, too. Maybe the restaurant.

So, that's where we go. Two blocks over and two blocks up. I know these streets by heart. I have my little map, but I don't need it. Good thing, because I wouldn't be able to see it in the dark of night. The cafeteria is shuttered and locked. I get a little closer to the door to see if there is a sign indicating opening time. Something tumbles out of the overflowing garbage bin and across my worn-out boot. I jump back, bumping right into my aunt. The sound of scampering feet increases. Rats!

We run for a block or so. Sort of. I can't make out the names of the streets. The gaslights, which are usually lit at dusk, have blown out long ago. But I have a feeling we're headed in the direction of my school. Maybe we can sit on the steps until Dennis Daly arrives. Yes, he'll let us use the washroom and rest a bit before we...what?

The high iron gate that surrounds the building is bolted shut. I pull it hard and then lean against it. Aunt Freda is standing on one foot and then the other.

"I've got to sit for a while. My legs are aching. Please, Fanny, isn't there a place to rest?"

I picture benches—the park.

"Hold onto me, Auntie, we have a few blocks to walk." Actually five until we reach Essex and Hester Streets. We walk slowly, leaning against each other, ducking into alleyways every time we hear a noise or see a shadowy figure.

At last, we arrive at the entrance to the park. My legs are hurting, too, and very shaky. I can't make out the outline of the benches, so I try to feel my way around. The first thing I touch is the cold wire fence. The second is someone's leg! A gruff voice calls out, "Leave me alone." The stench of stale alcohol enters my nostrils. I cough and turn my head away. Then I pull my aunt in a different direction.

I hear deep voices ahead of us. I stop and listen.

"Quiet night in the park, I guess because of the storm."

"Better for us. Let's take one more look around, and we'll head back to the precinct."

"Oh, no, it's the police," I whisper to my aunt, and we stand perfectly still. My eyes are closed and I'm holding my breath. Are they looking for us? Did Sophie send them? We listen as the cops' heavy steps circle a wide area, and finally exit just a few feet away from us. I pray they won't return tonight.

I collapse onto the bench behind us, pulling Aunt Freda down with me. Little rain water pools seep into the back of my skirt. I don't even care. My head is spinning. I wish I had somewhere to lay it down. I lean into the warmth of my aunt's arms, and let out a sigh. She shoves me so hard, I almost lose my balance.

"What are you doing?"

"What am I doing, Fanny? What have you done?" She gasps for breath. "It was bad enough that Sophie was throwing us out for no reason, but at least we could have left in the morning and then gone to Mike for help. It would have been all right, I'm sure...but *now*! Look at us, two poor souls alone in the dark on a wet park bench with no place to go...except maybe prison." She looks over her shoulder at the cold night sky.

"Sorry, Auntie, but I had to get the letter. I need to find out what's happening with Papa...and to let him know—"

"Let him know what, Fanny? That we're out on the street like two stray cats, without a roof over our heads?" She's sobbing. I reach over tentatively and gather her in my own arms. I can feel her body trembling with anger, or worry, or both. I wish I had a way to soothe her nerves. To take her away from our problems, if only for a while. I shut my eyes, and I envision what makes me happy: my classroom, my books!

"Auntie, remember my very first book, the one Miss Hall gave me?" No answer, just a few more sobs. "I showed it to you. You liked the picture."

She raises her head and nods slightly. "The one with of the girl with large eyes and long dark curls? What did you do with it, Fanny?" My aunt's voice is very quiet, but she's sitting up a little straighter.

"It's in my satchel. I couldn't read one word of it when I got it, and now I've finished the whole book."

"Maybe you can read it to me one day...if we ever have a chair to sit in...and a lamp to light the pages..." More crying. I reach out to her and hug her tight...so she can't get away.

"Listen, Auntie, It's too dark to read it now, but I remember the story so well. Let me tell you about the girl. Her name was Pandora."

I close my eyes for a moment to picture the pretty young woman. And I begin. "Once upon a time, long ago..." I'm imitating my teacher's voice when she tells us a story. "In the land of Greece, there appeared a woman, the first woman sent to earth by Zeus."

"Zeus?"

"This is a Greek myth, Auntie, *di mayse,* you know, a story."

"Ah, *de maysele,* keep going, Fanny. Go on with your little tale." I can feel her body relaxing a bit.

"Zeus, the god of the skies, sent this lovely, lively, and curious girl to live in a house containing a special box. Pandora was told never to open it. Never. Not even to think about opening it. For a while, she entertained herself, exploring her new home and gardens, and she was content. As she wandered from room to room, the box kept catching her eye. One day, she could resist no longer. She looked around to see if anyone was watching her. She thought, 'I'll just open it a crack and close it right away.' So she took the box in her two hands—"

"But she was told not to open it. She's like you, Fanny... she'll get in trouble."

"Well, that's exactly what happened."

"What do you mean?"

"She only wanted to take a peek. She meant no harm. Very slowly and carefully, she let her fingers lift the lid just a little bit. That's all she did. But something inside pushed it open all the way, and out flew a slew of ugly little creatures."

"What were they?"

"They were all the evils of the world: sickness, suffering, hatred, jealousy, greed, and other kinds of cruelties."

"You see, Fanny, she shouldn't have done that. She invited trouble, and it came."

"I know, but Pandora wanted to see. She tried to close the box top, but it was too late. The terrible things had escaped. Only one thing remained at the bottom."

"Did she let it out?"

"She did, once she realized what it was."

"What was it? Was this another mistake?"

"No, Auntie, it was good, the one thing that we all can have, that can help us most when times are bad."

"What on earth could that be?" Aunt Freda is now standing in front of me with her hands out, waiting for the answer.

"It's just what we need now...hope."

My aunt's eyes open wide. She places one finger under her chin and looks up to the sky.

"Hope," she repeats. "I hope, I hope for..." And, at that precise moment, the sun appears from just above the rooftops, and a new day begins.

TWELVE

The park is empty now, and quiet. There is a gentle breeze rustling the trees. Tiny droplets of water sprinkle the grass and my face. I wipe them away. I take a good look at the morning sky. It's going to be a better day... somehow. I rub my belly. "I'm hungry, Auntie."

She opens her change purse and carefully counts our few remaining bills and coins. "So we'll have breakfast. We have to eat, don't we? We'll need our strength today, for sure, for whatever—" Something is choking her words. My aunt rubs her chin and throat, up and down. This seems to help her find a stronger voice.

"Fix yourself, Fanny. No need to look like we're down on our luck." Aunt Freda presses my skirt with flattened palms. She straightens the collar of my blouse and looks up at me.

"Your hair is a mess. Come closer." She pulls her own comb through my hair, starting at the crown. It stops halfway.

"Ouch!" My hair is full of knots.

"This is not working. Let me look for my brush." She finds it at the bottom of her green sack, and pulls it out, along with a bunch of items that fall to the ground. I bend to retrieve a few embroidery needles, several packets of threads, a hankie...and a small card with printing on it. I can feel the raised letters, but I can't see them clearly. It's still too dark to make out the words. I place the assorted articles back into the bag, but I pocket the card. I'll take another look at it when we get to the tea shop.

I decide to avoid Hester Street. We don't want to run into Mendel or Sophie—or a band of policemen. I shudder at the thought. I don't need to look at the map that David drew for me. It is imprinted in my mind. And so are my memories of my good friend. I wonder how he is, and if he ever thinks of me. I would not like him to see what's become of us. He'd probably understand and maybe even try to help. But he's not here. He's in Chi-ca-go.

We have to keep away from Ludlow Street, too. We can't go to the factory...Sophie threatened to call the police if we showed up there, and also to complain about Mike to the boss. Sophie seems to think that Mr. Blum values her opinion. Somehow, I doubt that, but Aunt Freda says we shouldn't take a chance. So we can't ask Mike for a hand. The only hands we have at this moment are our own.

We walk down to East Broadway and several blocks over, to where Canal Street meets Allen. We make a right and head up to Delancey. The restaurant is buzzing. Our regular table is taken with a group of early risers, grabbing a bite before a long day of labor. I don't recognize any of the other diners, or the waiters. This is our usual place, but not our usual time, so it seems completely different.

We are given a small table in the corner. We shove our bags under our chairs and look around to see what is offered for breakfast. The hot, sweet tea, and the fresh rolls warm my belly, and I relax. A little. My aunt is counting out her coins. I search in my inside pocket for some loose change. I find a nickel, a penny, and the small card.

I hold it up to the light and try to make out the neat blue printing.

The Brandt Sisters

Ladies' Fashions: Custom Tailoring

12 East Fourteenth Street

New York City

I mouth the words.

"I can't hear you, Fanny, speak up."

"I'm reading this card, Auntie. It fell out of your sack."

"Let me have a look."

She holds it out in front of her, turns it over and back, and runs her fingers over the textured paper. "Yes, I think I know what this is." My aunt waves it in the air. "It's from the ship, from one of the three sisters. I gave her a handkerchief. She admired my stitching. She gave it to me just before we docked. I didn't know what it was, and I wondered why she gave it to me. And then, with everything that's happened since, it left my mind. And now, here it is." Aunt Freda holds the card in front of my eyes. "So what does it say?"

I clear my throat, and in my best speaking voice, I read the card. My aunt is scratching her head, so I explain it in Yiddish. I tell her it seems that the sisters we met on the ship have a business, right here in New York.

"Remember, Auntie, you said this was a fancy card. This looks like a shop for elegant customers. Clothing made to order, like in the Countess's magazines. That's why the sisters gave this card to you—they appreciated your sewing skills. Maybe they have a job for you. We'll go today!"

My aunt shakes her head. "I don't know, Fanny, they probably don't even remember me. Why would they? And we look

161

a fright after a night on the street. Maybe they won't let us in."

"Auntie, we have to go. We can't go back to work at Ludlow Industries, and we'll need money to get a place to stay. Let's give it a try. We have nothing to lose."

She straightens her back. "You're right, Fanny, and you'll come with me—"

"Of course I will."

We take turns washing up and changing our clothes in the tiny washroom. I glance around the restaurant, searching for a familiar face. We need to leave our bags somewhere. We can't go to the sisters looking like we're still traveling. I don't see anyone I know. More people are arriving. There is a line at the door. A waiter tells us that they need our table.

We lift our carrying cases and head out onto the street again. The sun is rising higher in the sky and shedding some warmth. I can hear the newsboys calling out the latest happenings. The pushcart vendors are starting to set up their wares. Aha! "Auntie, maybe Reb is here and will hold our bags for a while." She lets out a nervous sigh. I know, too, that this is not going to be an easy day. We have to find jobs and a place to stay. I don't know how, exactly, but we've already been through so much. I guess we can weather this, as well.

At first Reb seems pleased to see us, but then he shakes his head. "Shouldn't you be on your way to school, Fanny? And Freda, here so early? What's the matter?"

We pour out the complete saga of our troubles. He holds his head with both hands, ignoring any customers who approach. "I wish I knew of a place for you to stay. I, myself, rent a small room in a cramped apartment. But...I'll ask around." We tell him of our plan to see the sisters, and he agrees to keep our bags until evening. "Remember, Fanny. Be back here in plenty of time. We have to start clearing the streets by five o'clock. Sorry."

Before handing over her sack, my aunt reaches in for her change purse and a clean hankie. Then she pulls out a yellowed envelope. I stare at her. She's not looking at me. Actually, she's gazing at some point above the rooftops, and then down at what is in her hand. She puts it back into her sack and then takes it out again. Finally, Aunt Freda clutches the ancient letter to her chest. She lowers her eyes.

"One more thing, Reb. By any chance...I see you're a scholar. Perhaps you read Russian? I think this is..." She holds out the item in question. I look at her, and so does Reb. He opens the letter with great care and studies it for a while. "Yes, this is Russian. Very well written. I will tell you what it says." Reb has a very nice reading voice, too. Maybe he was a teacher in the old country. He translates the letter into Yiddish.

Dear Svetlana,

I didn't sleep at all last night. I had a big decision to make, and I'm not at all happy with my choice. But what could I do? I'm planning to leave this letter with Shayna, so that you will know my thoughts.

Last week, when I emerged from the woods, I overheard Mrs. Edelman gossiping with a customer. She was talking about you, Freda, and how foolish you were to be so indiscreet. She said that such behavior could ruin your reputation and cancel your impending marriage.

You never said that a match had been arranged for you, but maybe you didn't know. Life is so different in Moscow. I wasn't even aware of these village customs.

I would have liked to take you away with me to travel and study art. We could have lived as if we didn't have a care in the world. I realize that this cannot be. I have to make a living for my family, and you have obligations to yours.

I wish you well and hope that your intended will see the light in you. I will never forget it.

Freda, whatever happens, don't let anyone stand in the way of your brightness. You owe it to yourself to be happy and shine.
With fond memories and deep affection,
Misha

My aunt blushes a bit. She is hearing Misha's final words to her for the very first time. I give her a warm hug. Reb is watching Aunt Freda in wonder. She catches his expression and gives him a half smile. He looks like he's blushing, too. Aunt Freda remembers her manners. "Thank you, Reb, for your kindness. By the way, how many languages can you read?"

"How many? Well, yes...let me see." He starts to count on his fingers.

"First of all, Yiddish, Hebrew, of course, Russian, Polish, French, more or less, but not English. I was too old to learn when I got here and too busy trying to make a living. I should learn it, but I'm...tired."

"So many languages, and I can't read even one. It wasn't that I was too old, or too tired. It's that I was a girl and was never given the chance. I had no choice. In many things. But Fanny, here, she reads like a dream. English, of course."

That reminds me. "Reb, one more favor, please." I open my satchel and dig out Papa's letters.

"Please, could you read these, too? They're in Yiddish, I'm sure."

"Yes, certainly. For you—what's one more or less?" First he reads the opened letters.

Esteemed Mendel:
I hope this letter finds you and your dear wife in the best of health. I received information from your cousin Bertha that my sister-in-law, Freda, and my daughter Fanny may be staying in your home. I pray that this is so, and I thank you for your hospitality.

I am enclosing a letter to be read to Fanny, at your convenience. It is important that I communicate with her. May you be rewarded for your kindness.

With regards, Chaim Tatch

"There's another, should I read it, too?"

"Yes, please." I listen intently as he begins a longer letter.

"'My dear daughter,'" he says.

My eyes open wide.

Reb stops and looks at me. "Didn't Mendel ever read this to you?" I shake my head. "How could that be? But he gave it to you, no?"

I'm starting to perspire. "Er, in a way."

Reb looks down at the page. "A crime not to share this with you, Fanny. Imagine, a father's letter to his daughter from so faraway. *Di shande*, Mendel should be ashamed of himself. Well, let me continue. You've waited long enough."

I am writing to ask you to forgive me. Since when does a father request this of his child? I'll tell you. Since I got my senses back. It's been one month since your Uncle Avram's sister, Bertha, came to me with her cousin Sophie's address.

For days before that, Ida was running around complaining that you had not returned to take over the household chores. I told her that Freda probably needed you to stay for a while.

You can't even imagine what happened when we were told that you and your aunt were heading to America. Ida's fury was released. She screamed at me and then at poor Bertha. Ida accused us both of having been in on the plan.

She told me that I was a fool to have believed that your mother was a saintly woman. She told me to take a good look at Shira's family, which includes your Aunt Freda, an immoral kidnapper, and you, Fanny, an ungrateful brat, not worthy of her precious nephew. She ranted on and on until I thought my head would burst. I ran into my study to escape her tirade, and there I found Louie, curled up in my chair, crying his eyes out. He had heard everything.

It took all this to make me realize that I needed to be in charge again. I marched back into the parlor and told Ida that we were finished. I wanted her out of my home for good. She said she would never leave.

It's easy to blame Ida for all that had happened, but I must take responsibility for most of it. I was in too much of a hurry to remarry, thinking Ida would be a good mother to you and Louie, and a comfort to me. When things did not work out as I had planned, I'm afraid I lost heart and let her take over.

You turned out to be the brave one. Your mama, of blessed memory, always said you had a lot of spirit. I'm glad that you won't be marrying that useless pest. You deserve so much better. You were right. It's better not to rush. Look what happened to me. To all of us.

For now, Louie and I are living in your Aunt Freda's home and paying rent to Bertha. The rabbi is processing a divorce for me. I have put the house and my business up for sale. Ida will be given a financial settlement and be sent off to live with her sister. As soon as Louie finishes his studies, we will be leaving Vahivka. I will stay in touch with you through Mendel.

Until then, I trust you will be helpful to Sophie and responsible in all you do. Thank your Aunt Freda for taking good care of you. In spite of our past differences, I recognize that she is a strong and honorable woman. I send blessings to both of you.

Your devoted Papa

Reb looks up from Papa's letter just as a customer approaches. She seems to be in a big hurry. The woman reaches over me to shove her hand into the cart. She rummages through the variety of items. "Buttons, Reb, I need seven black ones, and some black thread."

"If you come back a little later, I'll look for you. Right now, I'm busy, you see."

The buyer glances at the bunch of papers and back at the wagon. "Can't you give me a minute? I need them now. What is this, a business or a post office?" Reb turns his back on the lady and turns his attention to the next note.

Dear Fanny,

Papa has said a lot to you in this letter, so I'll only tell you that I miss you very much. As you can see, a lot has happened in a short time, I think for the best. I hope, somehow, you will be able to let us know about your life in New York.

We are all right, for now. Mrs. Pirov comes here every day to clean and cook for us. I am studying a great deal in school. Papa has hired a special tutor for me. He is teaching me to read and write, and even speak some English. Papa says that after this school year, he will use the money from the sale of our home and his store to buy tickets for America. Some of my classmates have already left to join relatives there.

Maybe, one day, we will be together, again. Do you still remember how to make noodle pudding?

Love from your brother,

Louie."

Reb laughs now.

"Maybe you should send these letters to the *Daily Forward*." He holds up his copy of the Yiddish newspaper. Then he turns his attention to the latest letter. Reb brushes one finger over Papa's wax stamp and then opens the new letter with great care. He begins to read.

"*A cordial greeting to you, Mendel,*

I don't know if you received my previous letter, or if Fanny is with you now, God willing. I never received a reply from you, but I am trying again. I will make this brief. Louie and I will be sailing out of Bremen and arriving in New York shortly before Rosh Hashanah. So we will be there to celebrate the New Year with you. I am enclosing a note from Louie, and he will write the exact date according to the American calendar.

Regards,

Chaim Tatch

Reb holds up one more letter. He waves it in the air.

"Here it is! The very last letter for today!"

He takes a deep breath.

Dear Fanny,

I hope you and Aunt Freda are well. I have been missing you a lot and studying English, too."

He stops.

"The rest is not Yiddish, Fanny. Maybe it's English. Here, read it."

So, Louie really is learning English. I read this part aloud.

"Papa and I will begin our journey soon, and will arrive in New York Harbor on September 2. The name of the ship is SS Roland. *Please wait for us.*

Love from your brother,
Louie

Reb smiles at me. "So soon you'll have your papa and brother with you, Fanny. Good."

Good, yes, I think. *We'll all be together, just a few weeks from now, but where? We'd better start moving.*

My head is swimming with all the news from Vahivka—so much, all at once. My aunt is silent for quite a while. Her letter is not new at all. It contains words written over thirty years ago. But it's certainly new to her.

We walk off in the direction pointed out to us by Reb. I'm clutching the little card. It's small, but it might hold great promise. Maybe a good job for my aunt. Please. I've got to help make this happen. I look at Aunt Freda and notice that she appears *tsemisht.* The sisters mustn't see that she's confused. My aunt has got to show some confidence.

I take her hand gently, so as not to startle her. I keep my voice low, but firm. "Auntie, let's try to remember what the sister told you when she gave you this card." She's not listening to me. She's still lost in her thoughts. I raise my voice a bit, just as Miss Hall does when she wants her pupils to pay attention. I speak slowly, pausing between words. We walk slowly. She's staring at the ground. "Please, Aunt Freda, we've got to get it right." I pass the card in front of her eyes. "I *need* you to remember."

We stop, and I stare at her. She's still holding Misha's letter. I find my firm voice again. "Put it away, Auntie. You can think about the letter later."

She takes one lingering look at it and lets out a sigh. I watch as she folds it in half and half again. She buries it at the bottom of her sack. Her head is down. Her eyes are moist. She wipes them with one of her fancy hankies. "It's all right, Fanny. Now I know. Finally. The past is the past. But I wonder what if; I mean I wonder where..." She shakes her head, squares her shoulders, and lifts her chin. She marches off, saying, "No, no more wondering. This is a new day. Don't just stand there, Fanny. Give me the card." Aunt Freda runs her fingers back and forth over the engraved letters. "Mmm, let me think. Ai-m re-com, reco...I can't recall such strange words."

"Try again, Auntie."

"Ai-m reco-mendel."

"No, not Mendel—mended. I've got it. I am recommended. Yes, that's what she said. You know, Auntie...*rekomendrin*. They want you. We've got to say this to get in. It means that the sisters like your sewing skills, and they want you to work for them!"

"*Alluvai.*"

"I hope so, too."

The buildings get taller as we ascend. They are mostly brick, with many windows. By the time we get to Fourteenth Street, my neck is hurting from looking up and around. There's a lot to see. I notice that the streets are much cleaner than they are downtown. There are no clotheslines or push-carts in view. The one newsboy around is calling out only in English. My aunt is busy craning her neck as well. "So what's the latest news, Fanny?"

I wasn't paying attention to the boy, so I make up a headline. "Big news," I say, very seriously. "The talented seamstress, Freda Kasinoff, is heading uptown to secure a job with the Brandt sisters. She is recommended!" I start to laugh.

"Don't joke, Fanny, this is important. I've got to be serious."

She's right. I straighten my grin and look around. The people I see are serious-looking, too. And very well dressed. No headscarves or tattered shawls up here. Most ladies are wearing smart felt hats adorned with feathers or flowers. Short-waisted jackets skim over high-collared blouses that are tucked into well-tailored long skirts. Their shiny leather boots sport brass buckles or silver buttons. I glance down at my own shabby footwear. As soon as I have a few extra dollars, I'll buy myself a nice new pair. When will that be? I'm so busy looking at my shoes that I bump into a man.

"Sorry—I mean, excuse me—I wasn't looking. It's my fault." I use all the polite words I learned in school. The man is smiling. He looks as if he's dressed for business, wearing a gray pinstripe suit, a white shirt, and a blue tie. He's carrying a large leather briefcase. He has a very distinguished appearance, except for his ears. They stick out on both sides of his important hat. I try not to stare at them and focus instead on the gold watch, which is attached to his vest by a long chain.

"You're a polite young lady. I like that. Shouldn't you be in school by now?" His voice is deep. I like the way he enunciates each word.

"Yes, sir, I should be, but I had to skip class today. My aunt, here, is recommended for a job. I'm helping her." I show him the sisters' card.

He takes a good look at Aunt Freda, and then at me. He rubs his chin. "Yes, I see. Immigrants. The elders relying on the young."

I am blushing again.

"No need to be embarrassed, my dear young lady. Be proud. You're able to assist your aunt. That's good. But don't forget to return to your studies tomorrow. Your future is in your hands." And he rushes off.

Yes, I think, *that's what I've always wanted. To make my own way.* For now, getting work for Aunt Freda's hands is all I need to worry about.

Fourteenth Street is wide and bustling with horse-drawn carriages and trolley cars. I'm holding the card in my hands and consulting the numbers on each building. I find 11 East Fourteenth Street and number 13 next to it. What has happened to 12 East Fourteenth? Did it disappear? I can feel my aunt's anxious eyes watching me as I walk a few buildings to the right and left. I'm starting to worry, but I don't want her to notice. I have to think fast. Maybe the card is printed wrong. Maybe the sisters have moved away. Maybe there will be no job, no place to live, and no place for Papa and Louie. Tears are beginning to well up.

Where is the door that we need? I've got to keep searching. No, I need to ask someone. I look around. A few fancy ladies pass by. Their elegantly hatted heads are held high. They are busy chatting with each other in low voices. I let them go. My old shyness is returning, creeping up on me like a pesky fly. I close my eyes for a moment. I picture the annoying insect crawling up my sleeve, ready to whisper in my ear. Ready to tell me to go back downtown, to give up, to... what? I open my eyes wide and brush the imaginary nuisance off of me.

Then I get ready to take action. I march up the steps to 11 Fourteenth Street. I take hold of the heavy brass knocker and let it fall against the bronze plate. No answer. I turn to look at Aunt Freda. She's shaking her head. I bang two more times. I'm about to leave when I hear footsteps. A tall, narrow woman opens the door. She looks down at me. Her mouth is a straight line of disapproval. I run my fingers through my tangled hair and down my wrinkled skirt. I clear my throat and begin to speak—I mean, squeak. "Please, Miss, Mrs., I'm looking for—"

"Speak up, young lady, and state your business." Yes, my business. This is what we're here for. I remember how Miss James taught us to enunciate each word when we recite a poem. I try again.

"I am looking for this address." I hand over the card. The woman raises her eyebrows. "My aunt is recommended."

"Is that so?" I'm beginning to perspire. I shift my weight from one foot to the other.

"Well, I suppose..." She looks my aunt up and down, and she frowns. Then she points one skinny finger at a three-story building across the wide street. I thank our reluctant helper, head down the stairs, grab my aunt's arm, and pull her across the street. Now, I see, the numbers on this side are all even: ten, twelve, and fourteen.

Twelve East Fourteenth Street is made of brown-colored stones. The massive door is painted red. The golden knocker has a reassuring clang. A girl about my age answers the door. A starched, white linen pinafore covers her long black cotton dress. Her cap is of the same material as the apron. I can see that she's the housemaid, but even so, she looks at us in dismay. "I'm sorry; you must have the wrong—" She's about to close the door on us. I press it open with my elbow.

"My aunt, here, Mrs. Kasinoff, is recommended." The door pushes against me. This time, Aunt Freda holds out her arm. She towers over the little maid. Her voice is loud and clear. "I am reco-men-ded...reco-men-ded!" The girl steps back, and we walk right in.

We find ourselves in the center of a circular entry hall. A huge crystal chandelier looms high above us. There are several closed doors on either side. I can hear movement and voices from the room on my right.

I've always been a good listener. But in this case, I don't have to try too hard. The words that are escaping that room are too loud to ignore. First a woman's high-pitched voice.

"Why isn't this ready? I told you that the ball is tonight. Tonight!"

And a few modulated words in response. "Mrs. Whitfield, we are trying."

"Trying does not complete the gown."

"But Madame, you keep demanding changes. The seamstress cannot keep up with your requests." I hear a ripping sound and something like sequins or beads dropping to the floor.

The door is thrown open to reveal three women: one, half-dressed, standing on a raised platform; another on her knees, trying to sew a hem; and next to her, one of the Brandt sisters. It's the one with the glasses. She glances at us and then takes a better look.

Her eyes open wide, and she runs into the grand hall. She hugs Aunt Freda and then me. She takes a step back and rubs her eyes. "It's a miracle," she says to herself, in English. "The woman with the golden hands is here, just when I need her!" The sister takes one of my aunt's precious hands and leads her through the open door. The fancy lady is pulling at her unfinished gown and glaring at the girl beneath her. The seamstress is wiping her red eyes. The sister calls out, "Eileen!" The young maid appears. "Sorry, Miss Erna, they pushed their way in. I tried—"

"Never mind. It's fine. Here, take Marta and give her some tea. Close the door behind you. And ask Miss Pauline and Miss Beatrice to join me." She looks back at the angry client. "Don't worry, Madame, help has arrived. Your gown will be ready by six o'clock."

"I want it by five, on the dot, or I'll take my business elsewhere."

The sister wipes her brow and adjusts her glasses. By the time she looks up, my aunt is on her knees, straightening the hem on the unfinished garment. She takes a needle from a plump pincushion and selects the right color thread, a lovely shade of blue. Without a moment's hesitation, she pulls out the old stitches and begins her repairs.

"Is it OK that my aunt does this?"

"Yes, it's more than OK. You speak English now, and so well. We traveled across the ocean together, and I know how talented your aunt is, but I don't even know your names."

"My name is Fanny, Miss, and my aunt's name is Freda. You see, I've been going to school since we arrived and studying hard. I'm advancing."

The sister leads me across the room and over to a tall window. She seats me on a cushioned bench and lowers her voice. "So, Fanny, where have you been living?"

I look out at the wide boulevard. "With relatives."

"Of course. Fanny, this is important. Can your aunt stay today? This is an emergency of sorts, but we've been needing a good seamstress for a while. I'd be pleased to have her work here—or is she already employed? It's been a while, hasn't it? Almost two months."

I pause for a moment to collect my thoughts. "Aunt Freda has been doing finishing at an establishment downtown. They've been very happy with her work." I hope she doesn't ask why we're here today.

"Surely, they would be. She's a treasure. Let me have a few words with her. Has she learned any English?"

"Not too much, but she's trying."

"Then will you be so kind as to translate for me? Tell your aunt that I am offering her a job here, and I will pay her twelve cents an hour. Ask her to please stay to finish this gown, as soon as possible, and she will receive a cash bonus before she leaves tonight." I try not to show my relief. "Of course, certainly, Miss Erna."

174

By the time we approach my aunt, she is helping the lady out of her dress. It is full of pins and threads. I wait for the woman to depart before relaying the sister's offer in Yiddish. Aunt Freda's eyes open wide. She offers a hand to Miss Erna and almost drops the garment. She places it carefully on a table and smiles sweetly at her new boss. "Danke." She wipes her brow with one of her famous hankies. "Thank...you."

We seal the deal at tea. We are formally introduced to Pauline and Beatrice. The three sisters tell us how happy they are that Freda is going to work for them. My aunt eats quickly and returns to her task. I am encouraged to stay. They want to hear all about school and my plans, but I have to rush downtown. My aunt may have a new job, but we need a place to live. I've got to see the Reb. I excuse myself, telling the sisters that I am tutoring a little boy after school. They seem impressed. "Wait for me, Auntie. I'll be back for you this evening."

THIRTEEN

FRIDAY AFTERNOON

I don't know if it's the afternoon heat or the way I'm rushing downtown that's making me perspire. I can feel my damp blouse under my vest and jacket, but I don't have time to remove anything. I've got to keep going.

I get a chance to catch my breath while Reb is giving change to a customer. I wait for her to leave before telling him about Aunt Freda's new job. I hope he has good news for me, too.

He hands me two scraps of paper with an address on each one. "I've been asking around since you left. Here are two leads. Let me know how it goes, Fanny, and remember to be back by five. They'll make me pack up and leave."

I trudge up four flights on a dark, narrow staircase in a building on Delancey Street. I knock timidly at first and then harder. I hear a familiar whirring sound coming from behind the closed door. It opens to reveal a smaller version of Ludlow Industries. A little factory crowded into someone's living quarters. Five young women are working at sewing machines. Onions are frying in a pan on a black coal stove. A board covers the kitchen sink. A tall, thin man is bent over it, pressing pants with a heavy iron. A plump lady is stitching

177

in the buttonholes. She must be the finisher. But there is no sweeper, I see. The floor is littered with fabric scraps, bits of thread, and needles and pins. A toddler waddles around in the middle of this mess. He is followed by his mother. She is pulling her hair back and trying to secure it with a strip of cloth. It keeps falling over one eye. She pushes it back again as she heads over to stir the pot. She wipes her hands on her grease-stained apron and picks up the child. I must have the wrong apartment. I look at the address again. The mama calls out to me, "So you come for the bed?" Her English is broken. I don't know what other language she speaks, and I don't care. We just need a place to stay. I answer slowly. "May I see the room?"

It's not much bigger than our cabin in the SS *Bremen*, and certainly not as clean. Four narrow beds are stuffed into this tiny space. There is no sign of a dresser or night table. Clothes are piled on the ends of three of the beds. The other is bare and hardly big enough for one, let alone two. "That for you." She points to the empty one. One dollar a week, one bed and one dinner." I can smell the onions burning.

I'm on to the second address. This next one should be better. The good thing is that there are no stairs to climb. The apartment is on the first floor, convenient for us, but also for stray cats, insects, and any other intruder. The room for rent has a stuck window. It doesn't go down. There are only three beds in this room. One is occupied. I guess we can't be too fussy. Maybe the window can be fixed. And we'll have to share. What can we do? It's better than sharing a park bench. The other lady is probably nice enough. Did I say lady? The sleeping roommate turns over in bed, revealing a mustache and a full-grown beard!

The landlord says he takes in whoever has the money to pay. "This is America," he tells me, "and modern times, as well. If you're so particular about being separate, you should have stayed in the old country. That reminds me—I think the

Bravermans on the second floor have a spare room." I'm up the stairs in a flash.

A sweet elderly couple is sitting at the kitchen table. They could be anybody's grandparents back home. They are drinking tea from thick glasses. The man has a sugar cube between his teeth. The woman offers me a glass, too, in Yiddish, and I am happy to receive it. I sip slowly and let my cares slip away for a moment. I look around me. This is like a bit of home, right here in New York. I see a kiddush cup on the sideboard and a small bottle of wine. I can smell a challah baking in the oven. They are getting ready for the Sabbath. Yes, thank goodness, this is the perfect place.

But before I even get to ask about the spare room, two young women burst in with their traveling bags. Mr. Braverman tells me the room was rented to them just an hour before I arrived, and that they had gone to retrieve their belongings. Good for them. Lucky girls. Yes, Mama was right. Timing is everything.

Now I'm on my own. No more slips of paper to consult. No more recommendations. At least, I'm not sweating anymore. There is a chill in the air. The sun is beginning to sink down in the sky, along with my hopes. I'm holding back tears. I walk around for a while, wondering what to do. I think I hear someone behind me. I turn around. No one. Maybe I'm imagining things. I'd better hurry. I don't want to be late for Reb, and for my aunt. What will I tell her? We can't stay another night in the park.

My thoughts are interrupted by clanging bells—not the kind I hear in school. These are loud and insistent. This sound is accompanied by the clopping of horses' hooves and wheels bumping against the cobblestone streets. Then I see the fire wagon turn the corner at Rivington and Ludlow and stop. Policemen arrive on foot and block off both streets. I hear a gush of water and see smoke rising.

I turn in the other direction and try to figure out the best way to get to Ludlow and Grand, to Reb, as soon as possible. I don't have the map with me, the one David drew in my notebook, in what seems to be ages ago. But the image is imprinted in my mind. I raise my eyes and focus, as if I were actually reading it. I have to avoid walking near the factory or Sophie's apartment building. Who knows what kind of trouble awaits me in those places?

I rush along Rivington all the way to Allen and make a left turn. I pass our tearoom, and my stomach starts to murmur. When was the last time I ate something? I'd love to have a nice warm roll. Forget about that. No time and no money. Aunt Freda's purse contains the little we have left. I quicken my step, passing by Hester, down to Canal Street, across to East Broadway, and up Essex. The park is on the other side. I look away from the benches and pray that they won't be our beds tonight. I circle around Delancey and Orchard, really out of my way. I stop for a minute to catch my breath. I'm looking down at my worn-out boots. I'm exhausted. I hear my aunt's voice in my head. "Look up, Fanny, look up." And so I do.

At that exact moment, I see a man standing by the window of a small grocery store. He's hanging a white paper there—a sign. I cross the street to read it. The English words are printed in blue crayon: Rooms For Rent...Inquire Within. I rub my eyes and look again, to see if this is for real. It is. I straighten my clothes and hair a bit and push against the door. A ribbon of small bells ripples out a welcoming sound as I enter.

I've never been to this shop before, but somehow, it seems familiar. It's a bit like any other small grocery in our part of town. There's a long counter with a cash register. Next to it is a low stand with a pile of newspapers. Two rows of shelves contain canned goods and boxes of cereal and crackers. The lettering on these is in English. Some say, "Made in

Ireland," like David. And when the grocer speaks, he sounds
like David. "Yes, Miss, and how can I help you?"

"I'm here about the room. I see the sign in your window.
There is a room available, isn't there?" I'm beginning to sweat
again. I loosen my collar.

"Actually, there are two rooms. Where's your mum or
your dad?"

"I live with my aunt here in America. She's at work now,
uptown. I'm about to meet her there."

"So bring her around tomorrow, then, and let her have a
look."

"She trusts me to do this. Please, sir, may I see the rooms?"

"And how long have the two of you been living here, in
New York?"

"About two months, almost."

"And you speak English, so well—and read it, too, I see."

"I go to school." I straighten my shoulders and lift my
head. I feel proud of myself, even if we're having a hard time
now.

"Yes, that's a good thing, isn't it?"

I nod in agreement.

"Come along, then, and have a look at the rooms."

I follow him to the rear of the store. We pass by a large
stove and sink, and then a small alcove with an indoor toi-
let. The man tells me that the use of these is included in
the rent. A wooden door opens up to reveal a small sitting area, furnished with a round table and three straight-
backed chairs. A plump sofa covered in a worn flowered
fabric and an end table with an oil lamp complete this
room. What a lovely place to sit and read. Then there is a
bedroom, just big enough for a double bed and a clothing
wardrobe.

Nothing here is large or luxurious, but right now, it seems
like a palace! And the price for it seems out of reach, as well.
He's asking for five dollars a week! That's all that Aunt Freda

will make, including overtime. And me, without a job of any kind, now. Then I have an idea.

"Do you need help in the store, Mister? I can work after school, if you like, to reduce our rent. I'm a good worker."

"Hmm. Let me see. You read and write English, of course. Very good. And you know how to give correct change, right?"

I nod my head.

He points to a basket of bread and a cutting board. "Can you make sandwiches?"

I remember all the times I brought lunch to Papa in his store. "The best," I tell him.

"And I take it you know what a broom is for?" My mind flashes back to my first day at Ludlow Industries, with Sophie standing over me as I tried to sweep up all the scattered pins and fabric scraps.

"Yes, we're well acquainted."

"So, then, you'll be here every afternoon, from three to seven, and Sunday mornings, while I'm in church. Then the rent will be three dollars. That's the deal. You can pay me now, first and last week's—six dollars total—and I'll take the sign out of the window." He holds out his hand.

"As soon as I get back with my aunt, we'll pay you, I promise. She has the money."

The grocer scratches his head. "Well, then, make it soon, but I'll leave the sign where it is for now." He glances at the window, and at that exact moment, I hear the doorbells. They are welcoming in a couple and a young child. The father extends his hand to the grocer. He points to the sign, which is still in place. "I'm John Lean. We've come for the rooms. We have the cash."

He speaks just like David, too. A landsman. Maybe he'd like another Irishman to have the place. Bad timing for me. I could have sealed the deal a few moments ago if only I'd had the money in hand. I start to button my vest to leave, when I feel a bump in the seam. I walk over to the cutting board, and without even asking, I pick up the knife and use the point to rip out a few of Aunt Freda's careful stitches. One of Mama's ruby earrings catches the light and the eye of the grocer. He turns away from his countryman. "Please, mister, take the earring for safekeeping, until I return." He holds the jewel gently in the palm of his hand. He stares at it for a while. Maybe he's trying to figure out if it's worth the price of the rooms. I'm about to tell him how valuable it really is when I see a lonely tear appear in the corner of one eye. When he finally speaks, his voice is quiet. "This red stone brings to mind the ring my mum wore on Sundays. It was passed down to her from her old granny."

"This was my mama's, too."

"Well, then, I'll keep it safe for you, you can count on that." He places the ring in the cash register and shuts it tight. Then he turns to his countryman and offers his hand. "Sorry, Mr. Lean, but the girl was here first. I wish you well."

The grocer removes two keys from a hook on the wall. He tells me that the larger one is for the outside door, and the smaller for our rooms. He adds that his name is Liam Lynch, and that he and his wife, Liz, live upstairs, if we should need them.

"Thanks so much, Mr. Lynch. I'm Fanny, Fanny Tatch, and my aunt is Freda Kasinoff. We'll be back soon. Thank you again."

"Be sure to lock up after you're in for the night, Fanny. You'll start to work on Sunday morning, bright and early. There are aprons hanging behind the counter, and the price list is on the wall behind you." The little bells ring cheerily as I exit the place that will now be home. Thank goodness, and thanks to Mama's earring.

As I rush toward Reb's cart, I think I hear footsteps behind me, but when I turn around, there's no one near. I think I'm just tired. Reb is packed up and ready to leave. He's been waiting for me. I thank him and say we're all set. I'll tell him more tomorrow. I don't want to delay him further.

I hurry back to the store, open the front door, drop our bags, lock up again and head uptown to the Brandt Sisters' business. This time I am greeted by Eileen, who leads me into the fitting room. I enter just in time to see Mrs. Whitfield hugging my aunt!

"You, my dear, are a brilliant seamstress. I will be the envy of all my friends at the ball."

Aunt Freda is smiling a bit and shaking her head. I'll have to tell her later exactly what was said. Eileen carries the tissue-wrapped ball gown out to the lady's driver. As Mrs. Whitfield is helped into the waiting carriage, she turns to wave. "I'll be back for a new gown soon, and I want Freda. Only Freda. Good night, all."

Miss Erna looks at me as she tells my aunt how grateful they all are for the fine work. "You saved the day, Freda. Here is your well-deserved bonus. You can rest tomorrow. We'll see you Monday morning."

FOURTEEN

The large red door is closed behind us. I offer to help Aunt Freda walk down the stoop. Instead of taking my hand, she grabs my shoulders. "Fanny, was Reb able to help you find a place for us?"

"He tried, but..." My aunt steps back and reaches into her pocket. She counts out three crisp bills.

"It's all right, Fanny. I earned enough here for a night or two in a rooming house. Until we get a room for ourselves somewhere. I have a good job now. Don't worry."

"Auntie, the money you have will pay for one week—"

"What are you talking about, Fanny? You said that Reb couldn't help us."

"He did have a few leads for me. I'll tell you all about that later. After we get home."

"After we get where?"

"Come with me, Auntie, and you'll find out."

The walk back is slow. My aunt is tired, and so am I. But happy. Our shadows are getting longer, and the sky is darkening. At last we arrive. I stop in front of the window where I first read the sign. It's gone now.

"Fanny, why are we here? This store is closed for the night. We can get some food tomorrow."

"This is our home." I hold up the two keys. I insert the larger one into the padlock.

"Fanny, this is a grocery."

"I know, Auntie, and I'll be working here."

"But where will we live?"

I pick up our traveling bags and carry them through the store, past the stove and sink, and up to the wooden door. Then I use the smaller key to open it. I proudly show my aunt around our rooms. Her eyes, which were drooping with weariness before, are now open wide. Her mouth forms the letter O. She starts to speak and then stops. She walks back and forth from room to room, nodding and smiling. Then she comes over and hugs me tight.

"This is wonderful, Fanny! How on earth did you manage this? Let me rest a moment and catch my breath." She sits down on our sofa and continues to look around as I tell her about my day—the rooms that did not work out, the older couple's old-fashioned apartment, and the fire wagon blocking my way and leading me to the sign in the window. And then how I got myself a little job along with these rooms and then almost lost it all to the Irish family. I tell her how Mama's earring saved the day.

"You are a very clever girl. I'm proud to be your aunt, and grateful. Two wonderful rooms just for us, with furniture and a place to have our dinner." She walks over to the table. "What's all this?" A plump, round bread is resting on a wooden tray. It's bursting with raisins and covered with a mist of powdered sugar. An envelope is leaning against the loaf. I open it and pull out Mama's earring and a note. I read it aloud. *"Fanny, the bread is a welcome gift for you and your aunt. Take whatever groceries you need. You can pay me tomorrow or the next day. PS—I think that your precious earring is better off in your hands. Have a good night. LL"*

I take the earring into the bedroom with our belongings. We begin to unpack our bags for the first time in America. Somehow, we couldn't bring ourselves to do that at Sophie's. That was never home to us. When I get to the bottom of my satchel, I discover Grandma Faiga's candlesticks and the Sabbath cloth. That reminds us that this is Friday night, and we can celebrate here, in New York, in America, at last.

Aunt Freda and I wash up. I put on Mama's ruby earrings. This is a special occasion. My aunt covers her head with an embroidered scarf. She lights the thick white candles, lowers her eyes, and chants the ancient prayer. "Blessed art thou who has commanded us to kindle…"

The blessing is almost complete when I hear the sound of tinkling bells. Oh, my goodness! I forgot to lock the front door when we came into the store. I can feel the color draining from my face. I hear footsteps and then a man's voice calling out.

"Freda, Fanny, are you here?"

My aunt gasps. "Mike? Mike? How?"

I peek out from our partially opened door into the moonlit store. It *is* Mike…and the young boy, Hershel, from the factory. So that's who has been following me. And that's how Mike knew how to find us. He looks so relieved.

"Thank goodness you are well! I spent the entire day worrying about the two of you." Mike is looking directly at my aunt. "Sophie came to work today, claiming that you both left her apartment early this morning without a word of thanks or where you were headed. I didn't believe her for a minute, but I knew I'd never get the truth from her, so I sent Hershel out to look for you. He did a good job."

He hands the boy a few coins. Hershel thanks Mike and heads for the door. Just before opening it, he turns to look around. He smiles shyly and starts to speak. "Gut Shabbos to everyone. *A gute nacht.* I've got to go now. My mama's waiting for me." I can hear his voice is changing, like Louie's the last time I saw him. I take a better look at Hershel. He's so young and has to work hard for his mama and himself. I call out, "Hershel, you are welcome to come here sometimes. I know you don't have time for school, but I can teach you a little."

"A dank, Fanny. Thank you." He blushes and leaves.

I cut a hunk of cheese and weigh it on the scale. I write my name on the top of the pad I find on the counter, and I record the price. I do the same for a bottle of cider. I'll pay for everything on Sunday. My first sale.

Mike keeps his hat on as he recites the blessings over the juice and bread. Then we all sit down together to enjoy the first Sabbath meal in our new home. After dinner, we take turns telling Mike about how we were thrown out in the middle of the night and the scary hours we spent in the park. About finding the sisters' card and Aunt Freda's new uptown job.

Mike tells my aunt not to worry about Sophie, that she's just a bully with no real power. "Come back to work, Freda, we need you there. I'm sure I can get Mr. Blum to give you a pay raise. You certainly deserve it."

"No, Mike, I don't want to work in the same place with Sophie ever again, and I like the new job. Angela can fill in for me. She's good at finishing the garments."

Mike nods his head. "I do want the best for you, Freda, but I'll miss you. When will we see each other?"

My aunt gives him a big smile. "You found this place once, Mike. Maybe you can find it again."

Much later that night, I retire to the bedroom, leaving Aunt Freda and Mike to their conversation on the flowered sofa. I take my earring and put it away for another happy day. So many to look forward to: Papa's arrival with Louie, my graduations from grade school, high school, and beyond. And perhaps even a wedding (not my own for a long while). I lie awake in my warm bed, listening to Aunt Freda and Mike chatting, their voices rising and falling, as I drift off for the night.

$\mathcal{A}$CKNOWLEDGMENTS

$\mathcal{T}$hanks to those who have helped, encouraged, and inspired me along the journey of writing this novel: my husband, Edward Constain; our son, Bill and his family; writing teacher and mentor, Andrew Craft; fellow writers and friends, Anissa Bouziane, Brenda Serotte, and Gerda Walz-Michaels; Dr. Cory P. Frank.

I'd like to give special recognition to all teachers and librarians who help to educate our children and fulfill their dreams.

I offer a note of appreciation to the International Women's Writing Guild (IWWG), a wonderful organization dedicated to supporting women who write.

Made in the USA
Columbia, SC
29 March 2018